"For whom were you working?" Tom asked flatly.

Natasha's smirk deepened. "You don't want to know that, Tom."

"Don't say my name," he snapped. "You don't have that right."

Maddeningly, the smirk turned into a smile.

"For whom were you working?" he repeated.

"Everything is connected, Tom," Natasha said lightly. "It's all coming full circle."

"Oh, so now we're being cryptic," Tom snapped.

"You have to see the bigger picture. You have to look to the past to clearly see the future."

Don't miss any books in this thrilling series:

FEARLESS™

Available from SIMON PULSE

For orders other than by individual consumers, Simon & Schuster grants a discount on the purchase of **10 or more** copies of single titles for special markets or premium use. For further details, please write to the Vice-President of Special Markets, Pocket Books, 1260 Avenue of the Americas, New York, NY 10020–1586, 8th Floor.

For information on how individual consumers can place orders, please write to Mail Order Department, Simon & Schuster Inc., 100 Front Street, Riverside, NJ 08075.

FEARLESS™

FREAK

FRANCINE PASCAL

SIMON PULSE
New York London Toronto Sydney Singapore

This book is a work of fiction. Any references to historical events, real people, or real locales are used fictitiously. Other names, characters, places, and incidents are the product of the author's imagination, and any resemblance to actual events or locales or persons, living or dead, is entirely coincidental.

First Simon Pulse edition November 2003

Copyright © 2003 by Francine Pascal

Cover copyright © 2003 by 17th Street Productions, an Alloy company.

SIMON PULSE
An imprint of Simon & Schuster Children's Publishing Division
1230 Avenue of the Americas, New York, NY 10020

 Produced by 17th Street Productions,
an Alloy company
151 West 26th Street
New York, NY 10001

All rights reserved, including the right of reproduction in whole or in part in any form.
For information address 17th Street Productions, 151 West 26th Street, New York, NY 10001.

Fearless™ is a trademark of Francine Pascal.

Printed in the United States of America
10 9 8 7 6 5 4 3 2 1

Library of Congress Control Number: 2003109086
ISBN: 0-689-85767-5

To Daniel Stokes

My name is Gaia Moore, I'm seventeen years old, and for the first time I can remember, no one is trying to kill me.

I know what you're thinking: I'm a schizophrenic paranoid delusional. This is not a normal thing for a seventeen-year-old girl to say. But that's just it. I'm not a normal seventeen-year-old girl. I wasn't normal at fifteen or ten. The last time I remember knowing that I was safe was when I was about eight, making mud pies in the backyard in the Berkshires, my knees covered in Rugrats Band-Aids. But even then I wasn't safe—I just didn't know it yet.

I've never had a normal life, and that's all I ever wanted.

I wanted afternoons filled with soccer practice instead of tactical training. I wanted my mother to live long enough to hear about my first kiss. I wanted a father who was around to read me bedtime stories every night instead of disappearing for days at a time. All I wanted was an existence that even vaguely resembled those of the well-adjusted ballerinas and spelling-bee champions and hopscotch experts around me.

But I could never have that. Someone in my family was always in danger. Someone was always trying to kidnap me or experiment on me or—you know—kill me. My mother was murdered. My father has been presumed dead more times than I can remember. I've had friends beaten and shot and stabbed. My first boyfriend almost died because of me.

Nothing was ever normal. Until now.

This is what normal feels like. I don't have to sit around wondering what Loki's going to do next, because he's gone—buried somewhere inside my uncle Oliver's subconscious. I don't have to spend my time trying to think like Natasha or Tatiana to figure out their strategy, because they're in custody. We still don't know who kidnapped my dad and took him to Russia, but the CIA is working on it, and for now, he's home. With me. Me and Dad, living together, alone. Like we're supposed to be. Like a family.

So there's no reason to obsess. No reason to plan and plot and chase and spy. I don't even have to train. I don't *have* to do anything.

This is what normal feels like.

I don't know what to do with myself.

To: Y
From: X22
Subject: Prisoner 352, Codename Abel

There has been a security breech in sub-sector K. Prisoner 352 is AWOL. Unconfirmed reports state that a young woman, believed to be Genesis, along with two men were instrumental in the liberation of 352/Abel. They are believed to be en route to the States, if not already there. We await your orders.

All is well, Gaia thought, taking a deep breath. She almost didn't dare to **a perfect** believe **moment** it, but it was true.

GAIA MOORE WAS HAVING A MOMENT
she'd probably remember for- **"So,**
ever. She was one of those rare
people who had these burned-
in-her-memory moments all
the time, but this one was dif- **listen . . ."**
ferent.

This one was good.

Good memorable moments were atypical in Gaia's
particularly screwed-up life. The awful ones, those
came up all the time.

Like the moment she learned her mother was
dead. The moment she realized that the man she had
always thought was her father might actually be her
evil uncle, Loki. The moment Mary passed away. The
moment Sam was kidnapped. The moment that Loki
operative fired shots at Ed. The list of gut-wrenching,
miserable, devastating moments went on and on.

But these light, content, all-is-right-with-the-world
moments? They were very few and very far between.
And when she realized she was having one, instead of
automatically thinking of the few things that were still
wrong—things that could crap all over the moment
like a giant pigeon—Gaia just smiled.

For once she was going to let herself be
happy.

"I like this," Jake Montone said, lying back next to
her on the big mound of rock near the Columbus

Circle entrance to Central Park. "Who would've thought there was actually a place in this city where you could see stars? Actual ones, I mean. Famous people I've been seeing everywhere lately. It's like you get one warm day and they suddenly come out of hiding. I was almost nailed by Brad Pitt on Rollerblades this afternoon in Union Square."

"Jake?" Gaia said, the back of her skull searching for a smooth bit of stone to rest on.

"Yeah?" he asked. He turned his head so he was looking at her profile.

"Shut up," she said.

"Right."

Ever since Gaia, Jake, and Oliver had returned from their little smash-and-grab job in the former Soviet Union (they'd smashed a fortress and grabbed Gaia's dad, Tom), Jake had been prone to these little fits of verbosity. Just every once in a while. Like he was a little kid that was still psyched up by a trip to an amusement park and couldn't contain his excitement. Gaia would never admit it, but somewhere deep down she kind of thought it was cute. In an irritating sort of way.

A jagged point bit into the back of her head and she moved again, sighing in frustration. Jake sat up, slipped out of his denim jacket, bunched it into a ball, and moved to prop it under the back of her head. For a split second Gaia thought about refusing, making a crack about his chivalry and turning it into a joke, but she stopped herself. Instead she just lifted her head, then leaned back into the Jake-scented softness.

Ah. Pillow. Just one more thing to make the perfect moment last.

All is well, Gaia reflected again, taking in another deep breath. She almost didn't dare to believe it, but it was true. Her father was home, safe and sound. Her uncle had been living for days now as good old normal Uncle Oliver with no signs of Loki-ness whatsoever. There was no one out there hunting her down, tracking her every move, plotting ways to take her out.

And to top it all off, she had a new friend. A real friend. Surprisingly enough Jake Montone had turned out to be, contrary to all snap judgments, a non-moron. He was, in fact, freakishly true. Supportive. Noble almost.

"I can't believe that guy actually gets to have sex with Jennifer Aniston," he said suddenly, his brow furrowing beneath his tousled dark hair.

Okay, so he was also still a guy. But he had already saved Gaia's life, accepted her increasingly psychotic family situation with only pertinent questions asked, *and* dropped everything to come to Russia with her to save her father. In a short time he'd gone beyond the call of duty, friendship-wise. He'd gone beyond the call of duty for a damn guardian angel.

"So, anybody at school ask where you were for the past few days?" Jake asked.

"Not really. The teachers are used to me disappearing, and no one else in the world notices."

Except Sam, Gaia thought, her heart giving an extra-hard thump. *Sam noticed.* Sam had noticed to the tune of eight messages on her answering machine. Gaia had been more than a little surprised when she heard his voice over and over and over again on the tape. The last time she'd seen the guy he'd basically told her to get out of his life and stay out. By the time she was done listening to his messages it was fairly clear that he wanted the exact opposite.

I need to call him back, Gaia thought. But even as her brain formed the suggestion, the rest of her felt exhausted by the mere thought. The last thing she wanted right now was to open a can of emotionally wrought worms. She'd much rather just stay where she was—lying on her back in the park, staring at the sky, with Jake's warmth next to her, keeping the goose bumps at bay.

"What about your dad?" Gaia asked. Jake had been staying with Oliver since their return from Russia. Oliver needed to make sure no one was watching Jake's building. There was no way Jake's father was still buying any "I'm just staying at a friend's/there's a last minute school trip/my dog ate my homework" excuses any longer.

"Luckily Dad had to go out of town for some physicians' conference," Jake said. "He left before I got back and he doesn't even realize I haven't been home." He pulled his tiny cell out of the front pocket of his jeans and checked the screen. "The beauty of the cell phone."

"Nice," Gaia said.

"Besides, Oliver says I can go back tonight," Jake told her, replacing the phone after scrolling through a few text messages. "He gave the all clear."

"I'm glad," Gaia said sincerely.

"So, listen," Jake said, propping himself up on his elbow and turning on his side.

Gaia swallowed and her stomach turned. It was a loaded "so listen." The kind that was usually followed by either an unpleasant announcement like, "So, listen, I'm moving to Canada." Or by an awkward-silence-inducing question like, "So, listen, do you want to go to the prom?" Not that Gaia had ever been asked to a prom before, but she could still identify the appropriate "so, listen."

She stared at the sky and held her breath, waiting for the ax to fall, not sure of which ax would be the quicker, less painful one. Gaia had been getting the more-than-a-friend vibe from Jake for a few days now, but she'd chosen to ignore it. Mostly because acknowledging it would require acknowledging the fact that she was also attracted to him and Gaia was definitely not ready to go there.

Not just yet.

Whenever she allowed herself to admit she liked a guy, only anguish ensued.

"I was wondering if you might want to—"

Jake's question was interrupted by a sudden, blinding light that was directed right into his eyes. He held up his hand to shield himself and the beam moved to Gaia's face. She squinted against the stinging pain and sat up, her boots scraping against the grainy surface of the rock.

"What do you kids think you're doing out here at this hour?" an authoritative voice asked.

The light finally moved away and Gaia was able to distinguish the outlines of two NYC police officers through the pink dots that were floating across her vision.

"Just hanging out," Jake said, pushing himself to his feet. He was slightly taller and more than slightly broader than either of the men in blue.

"Yeah, well, it's not the safest place to *just hang out* these days," the chubbier of the two cops said, eyeing Gaia as she stood. He shone his light along the ground, looking for beer cans, crushed joints—anything that could allow him to give more than the usual amount of hassle to Jake and Gaia.

"We've had a number of attacks in this area of the park in the past few days," Cop Number One said. "I suggest you two move it along, for your own safety."

"Sure," Jake said, leaning down to grab his jacket. "No problem, Officer."

He used his jacket to nudge Gaia's arm and they turned and scrambled down the side of the boulder. Gaia sighed as she fought for her footing on the steep side of the rock. She appreciated what the cops were trying to do, but they'd obliterated her perfect moment. Of course, they may have also saved her from an awkward, embarrassing, tongue-tied conversation with Jake about his "so, listen." Little did they know they'd just added "rescue from ill-fated romantic interludes" to their duties as New York's finest.

Gaia jumped the last few feet to the ground and landed next to Jake. He shoved his arms into his jacket and straightened the collar as they started to walk. For a few blissful seconds there was total silence—aside from the faint honking of car horns somewhere out on the streets that surrounded the park.

Then, Jake tried again. "So, anyway, as I was saying—"

"Hey! No! Help! *Help!*"

It took Gaia a split second to realize that she wasn't hearing her own desperate get-me-out-of-here pleas, but actual shouts of panic.

"It's coming from over there," Jake said, taking off.

Gaia was right at his heels, slicing through toward what sounded like a struggle. They suddenly emerged into a small clearing and saw not one, but two middle-aged women in jogging suits, flattened on their backs by four men in jeans and do-rags. Two of the men were each holding a woman down and two of the men were yanking at each of their clothes.

Gaia took one look at the tearstained and desperate face of the woman closest to her and felt her fingers curl into fists.

"Hey!" Jake shouted at the top of his lungs.

All four men stopped and whipped their heads around. At the instant of surprise, Jake and Gaia both launched themselves at the clothing-gropers and tackled them off their victims. As Gaia tumbled head over heels with her man, she saw the two women struggle to their feet.

"Go!" Gaia told them, flipping the assailant over and digging one knee into his back. A second guy wrapped his arm around her and yanked her off his friend. "Get out of here!" she screamed at the joggers.

The stunned, shaken women seemed to come to at that moment and they wisely ran. Gaia was thrown away from her second man and she had to fight for her balance. As soon as she found her footing again, she got her game face on. Jake was working his best *Matrix*-worthy moves on his two guys as Gaia's men circled, leering at her.

"We got the girl, Slick," one of them said, punctuating his statement by spitting at her feet. "Aren't we lucky?"

Slick looked Gaia up and down slowly. "You said it, buddy."

If you're feeling so lucky, come and get me, Gaia thought. *Quit wasting my time.*

Slick came at her then with a clumsy one-two punch, which she easily blocked. She thrust the heel of her hand up into his nose, waited for the satisfying crack and the spurt of blood, then turned around, hoisted him onto her back and over her shoulder. He landed on the ground in front of her, clutching his nose, rolling back and forth and groaning in pain.

Gaia looked up at his friend and lifted her eyebrows. "Ready?"

He let out a growl and ran at her. Gaia was about to throw a roundhouse at him when Jake shouted her name. She looked up at the last second and saw a third guy coming at her from her left. Glancing at their trajectories, Gaia quickly ducked, crouching as low to the ground as possible. She smiled when she heard the *thwack,* then stood up and slapped her hands together.

Both of the thugs were laid out on the ground, unconscious. They'd smacked heads coming at her and knocked themselves out. It was almost too easy.

"Amateurs," Gaia said under her breath, stepping over one of the bodies.

"Nice work," Jake told her, reaching out his hand. They high-fived and Gaia noticed that the fourth guy was also unconscious, crumpled into a seated position against a tree.

"You, too," she said.

They looked up when they heard rustling in the dark and the huffing and puffing of approaching men. The two cops that had roused them from the boulder came skidding into the clearing, hands on their holsters. They took one look around at the men on the ground, then gazed at Gaia and Jake, stunned.

"What happened here?" Chubby Cop asked, looking impressed against his will. "I thought we told you two to move along."

"And we did," Jake said, opening his arms. "You're welcome."

Cop Number Two shot Jake a wry smile as he knelt down to cuff Slick. "And now you can hang out while we get your statements, wise guy," he said.

Gaia and Jake exchanged a quick smile and leaned back against a thick tree trunk to wait. The side of Gaia's shoulder pressed into the back of Jake's and she didn't move away.

"They're gonna take credit for this, aren't they?" Jake whispered.

"Probably," Gaia replied.

"Figures. I feel like Batman. I keep kicking ass and there's no one I can tell about it," Jake said. Then he smiled and nudged his shoulder back into hers. "'Cept you."

Gaia felt the corners of her mouth tugging up slightly. What was wrong with her? Was she actually *enjoying* flirtation?

"So, Gray's Papaya after this?" Jake asked as the

cops roused the two knuckleheads that had run into each other.

Gaia's stomach grumbled. "Definitely."

She tucked her chin and turned her face away from him, smiling for real. She'd been doing this forever—beating up toughs in the park, ducking from or dealing with cops, then going for a post-fight midnight snack. But she'd been doing it forever alone. And she'd always thought that was the way she liked it. Yes, actually. That was the way she *had* liked it.

But now. . . now she liked having someone there. She liked having Jake to share all this with. She liked having an. . . ally.

Huh. Maybe it's true, Gaia thought, an evening breeze tickling a few strands of her long blond hair against her face. *Maybe things* can *change.*

TOM MOORE SAT AT THE SMOOTH metal table and glared across at the prisoners. His spine was straight, his fingers clasped into a knot, his elbows just slightly off the edge of the table-top. He breathed in and out deliberately, maintaining his composure—maintaining his calm.

Venom

Just another set of criminals. Just another day.

"Are you going to say anything?" Natasha asked.

"I'll ask the questions," Tom spat back instantly. He could taste the venom in his own mouth.

Just another set of criminals. Just another day.

Tatiana blinked but remained otherwise impassive. She looked small and wan, her light skin translucent and green in her bright orange jumpsuit. The monstrous cuffs circling her tiny wrists were almost comical. Even though it was impossibly cold in the interrogation room, there was a line of sweat visible above her upper lip. It was taking a lot more effort for Tatiana to remain composed after days of stony, obstinate silence in her cell. Far more effort than her more experienced, more world-weary, more spy-game–weary mother.

Tom shifted his gaze to Natasha again. Her dark hair was pulled back in a low braid that hung heavy and smooth down her back. She wore an amused smirk on her face. The face he had once held, once kissed, once touched with the tenderness that he'd formerly reserved only for his wife—his one true love.

An acidic bitterness shot through his stomach. He could only hope his nausea couldn't be detected by the detainees.

"That's fine," Natasha said finally, shifting slightly in her iron chair. "It's just that you're not. Asking questions, that is."

"For whom were you working?" Tom asked fl

The smirk deepened. "You don't want to know that, Tom."

"Don't say my name," he snapped. "You don't have that right."

Maddeningly, the smirk turned into a smile.

"For whom were you working?" he repeated.

"Everything is connected, Tom," Natasha said lightly. "It's all coming full circle."

"Oh, so now we're being cryptic," Tom snapped.

"You have to see the bigger picture. You have to look to the past to clearly see the future."

Tom clenched his teeth. She was trying to make him think about Katia, trying to make him crack. But Katia was not just his past. She was his past, his present, his future. Why he'd ever let himself lose sight of that, he had no idea.

"For whom were you working?" Tom repeated once again, glaring at her.

"I want to talk about a deal," she said.

Tom got up and threw his chair across the room, the noise slicing his eardrums as it clattered and crashed. Tatiana flinched as he leaned his knuckles into the table and got right in Natasha's face.

"You tried to kill my daughter! You tried to *kill* Gaia! And you have the audacity. . . the unmitigated *gall* to sit here and talk to me about a *deal!?*" he shouted, his eyes so wide they felt about to burst.

She didn't move. She didn't blink. And suddenly

Tom Moore knew. He knew that he was going to grab her. He saw his hands around her throat. Saw himself choking the life out of her. Who would blame him if he did it? The woman was sitting here talking in code, making up riddles, and she'd tried to murder the only family he had left. She deserved to die.

"Agent Moore!"

The door to the cinderblock-walled room flew open and Director Vance stood on the threshold, his intimidating former–Navy Seal, former–NCAA basketball player frame blocking out the light from the hallway. He pressed his full lips together into a thin line.

"That's enough, Agent Moore," Vance said in his rumbling baritone.

Tom didn't move. His knuckles turned white against the table as he continued to glare into Natasha's unwavering eyes.

I told this person I loved her. I thought I was going to be with her forever, he thought. The visions he'd had of himself and Natasha together—of making a family with their daughters—flitted through his mind, whirling together in a sickening tornado of colors.

"Agent Moore, I'm not going to ask you again," Vance said, stepping into the room.

The whirlwind suddenly stopped. Tom swallowed hard and struggled to focus on Vance. Ever so slowly, some semblance of balance returned to his mind and he realized what he was doing. He was letting Natasha get the upper hand. He was letting her have the whole game. He smoothed down the front of his blue suit jacket, hoping to regain some shred of dignity.

But when he glanced at her again it was clear from the expression of triumph on her face that all was lost. He couldn't handle being around her. And he'd just proven it.

Tom turned and followed his director out of the room and into the monitoring space just beyond. A couple of agents stood in front of the one-way glass that looked over the interrogation room and they averted their eyes when Tom entered. The second the door was shut behind him, Vance turned on Tom, his dark eyes livid, his deep brown skin flushed with anger.

"Moore, don't you *ever* let me see you lose your cool like that with a prisoner again, you understand me?" Vance spat, leaning in over Tom. "You know what you were in that room? You were that prisoner's bitch!"

Tom pulled his head back slightly, unaccustomed to such severe scolding after his glorious tenure in the CIA. Still, he knew on some level that Vance was right. There wasn't much he could say.

"I'm sorry, sir," he said, swallowing his pride. "It won't happen again."

"Damn right it won't. Because you're going home," Vance said through his teeth.

It took Tom more time than absolutely necessary to process this. The man couldn't be suggesting that he was being taken off this case. Didn't Vance know how invested in this he was? He had to find out who had kidnapped him, who had ordered his daughter to be killed. He had to find out for sure whether or not his brother, Oliver, was involved as he so highly suspected.

"What?" Tom spat out finally. "No! Sir, I—"

"You heard me, Moore," Vance said. "These particular prisoners obviously have you more than a little on edge." He paused for a breath and looked at Tom sorrowfully, almost pityingly. "You're taking a little time off," he added, causing Tom's heart to sink with the finality of it all. "Starting now."

GAIA OPENED THE DOOR TO THE

Out with he Old. . .

72nd Street apartment on Friday after school and immediately went on alert. There was a crash coming from Natasha's—no, her *father's*—bedroom. She and Jake looked at each other. There was someone else there.

Her first instinct was to call her father's name and see if it was him. But what if it was an intruder? Then she'd just end up calling attention to herself and Jake. Gaia tiptoed toward the living room, her rubber-soled boots soundless on the hardwood floor.

Footsteps approached, confident and loud and not remotely trying to be stealthy. Gaia flattened herself against the nearest wall, around the corner from the hallway. That was when her father emerged into the room, all smiles.

"Hey, honey!" he said, shuffling a few envelopes in his hands. His dress shirt was unbuttoned at the top and the sleeves were rolled up above his wrists. "I didn't hear you come in!"

His eyes flicked to Jake, who was now standing outside the door to the kitchen, his muscles visibly slackening.

"Hello, Jake," Tom said as Gaia forced her fingers and her jaw to unclench.

Her father breezed by her and sat down at the head of the dining room table where there were dozens of neatly arranged piles of bills and papers. He started pulling papers out of the envelopes, sorting them, and tossing the envelopes into the kitchen garbage can.

Gaia eyed her father. This was all very weird. Not only was he home in the middle of the day, but he was doing paperwork—something she hadn't seen him do. . . ever. When her mom was alive, that was her territory, and since then her father had never been around for enough days in a row to even know that there *were* bills.

On top of it all, there was an odd air about him. He was humming. His knee was bouncing under the table. Her father was normally cool, aloof, sometimes intense, but always in a quiet way. Just then he was acting, well, hyper.

"Dad?" Gaia asked, tucking her hair behind her ears. "Everything okay?"

"Fine. Great, actually," he said, glancing up at her for a split second before returning his attention to the papers.

Jake moved into the room, stuffing his hands into the front pockets of his jeans and giving Tom a wide berth. Gaia could tell that Jake sensed something was up.

"I heard a crash in the bedroom," Gaia said, sitting down in a chair across from her father. She pulled her messenger bag off over her head and laid it on the floor.

"Right, I broke a lamp," her father said. "I'll clean it up later."

Gaia looked at Jake and he tilted his head, giving her a look that said, *"He's* your *father."*

"Okay, so what are you doing home?" Gaia asked, glancing at her black plastic watch. "It's four o'clock."

"I decided to take some time off," Tom said, slapping a piece of paper down on top of a pile. Her father taking time off? Was this some kind of new, previously unexplored reality?

"What? But Dad, what about Natasha and Tatiana? What about your kidnappers? You can't just—"

23

"But I am," he said calmly. "My director thinks I need to take a break and I agree."

He was lying. She could tell by the way his jaw was tensing, making his cheek bulge slightly. He didn't want to take time off—his director was making him. This was insane. How were they supposed to find out who had kidnapped him if they weren't even going to let him interrogate the two people who *might* give them a lead?

"We're both going to have to let the CIA do their job," her father said, reading her distraught expression perfectly.

Gaia had no idea how he could be so accepting of this. Her father wasn't a quitter; he was a fighter—just like her. She wasn't going to just drop this investigation. She'd do it on her own if she had to, no matter what the CIA or her father said. Whoever had kidnapped her father had to be found and be brought to justice.

"In the meantime there's something I wanted to talk to you about," her father said with a forced smile. "How would you feel about making a new start?"

"What kind of new start?" Gaia asked slowly, still adjusting to his new attitude.

"Should I—" Jake asked, motioning toward the bedrooms.

"No, stay," Tom said with a laugh. "I just wanted to ask Gaia if she'd like to do a little shopping this weekend."

Gaia's jaw dropped, but she recovered quickly and snapped it shut again. That was definitely a phrase she never thought she'd hear. Not from her father, anyway. The things she heard most often from him were phrases like, "Stay off the radar," "I'll try to be in touch sometime next month," and "Aim for the solar plexus."

"Shopping?" Gaia asked, slumping back in her seat. "For what?"

Please don't let him say bras or something like that, Gaia thought. *Like he suddenly wants to make up for not being there and for my not having a mother.*

Gaia didn't blame her father for his many disappearing acts over the years—at least not anymore—not now that she knew what he was doing on all those excursions and why. He was fighting the good fight. Protecting her. Protecting the free world. It had taken Gaia a long time to accept that and move on. She couldn't handle it if he decided to take on the role of guilt-ridden father now.

"New furniture," Tom said. "Everything in this place belongs to Natasha and Tatiana. I think it's time we get some of our own things, don't you?"

A little stirring of excitement came to life in Gaia's chest, quelling the determination for revenge ever so slightly. She hadn't thought of it that way, but her father was right. This place was going to be their home. Their home. She and her father hadn't had one of those in years. Why would they want it to be decorated by their evil archenemy?

"Really?" Gaia said, too unaccustomed to the idea of doing something as normal as furniture shopping with her father.

"Yes, really," Tom said, standing. He moved over to the end of the hallway and looked off toward the opposite end—toward the room Gaia once shared with Tatiana. "We can get rid of those two beds and get you a double. . . move out that old-fashioned desk—I'm guessing it's not your style," he added with a grin.

Gaia liked what he was saying, but the way he was saying it was still odd. Almost manic. He was too excited about the prospect of shopping.

He wants to be at work, she thought with total certainty. *He wants to find his kidnappers as much as I do, but they're freezing him out.*

Well, maybe her father needed a little normalcy after everything he'd been through. And if so, she'd help him get it. But in the meantime, she'd do a little digging of her own.

Gaia sat up straight and squared her shoulders. "Okay, I'm in," she said. "Actually, we can go tomorrow. We have the day off for some teacher's conference."

"Good. Tomorrow it is," her father said, squeezing both her shoulders from behind. "We'll go over to Seventh and hit the stores." He turned, hands in the pockets of his khakis, and looked around the living room. "It'll be a whole new start. Out with the old, in with the new."

Gaia smiled slightly and looked up at Jake, who was staring right at her. She felt a flutter in her heart as their eyes locked. Maybe Jake could help her with her investigation. She was clueless as to where to start, but maybe they could figure that out—together.

A whole new start, she thought. *Out with the old, in with the new.*

OLIVER SAT IN ONE OF THE FEW

Rejection

chairs in his brownstone in Brooklyn, staring at the telephone on the table next to him. A half-empty bottle of scotch reflected the glow from the desk lamp that afforded the only light in the room. He took a swig from his glass and braced himself as the warm liquid burned down his throat.

It's just a phone call, he told himself. *You've taken phone calls from the President of the United States in your day. Just get it over with.*

He placed the tumbler down, picked up the receiver, and quickly punched in Gaia and Tom's number. He had no idea why he was overcome with such trepidation. Yes, there was a lot of bad history between him and his brother and niece, but that had all changed. They had fought side by side in Russia. They had escaped together. And even if he and Tom had been at each other's throats half the time, going through those experiences together had brought them closer. He could feel it. Tom must have been feeling it, too.

The phone rang a few times and he finally heard someone pick up at the other end. Oliver started to smile.

"Tom Moore," his brother said stiffly.

"Hello, Tom. How are you settling in?"

Silence. Oliver's heart thumped almost painfully.

"Tom?"

"I don't want you calling here again," his brother said, his tone impossibly cold.

"Tom, please. I just thought you and Gaia and I could get together," Oliver said, sitting forward in his seat. "To talk things over... maybe have a meal—"

"Until I know with absolute certainty that you had nothing to do with my kidnapping and with the threats to Gaia's life, I have nothing to say to you. And I don't want you contacting her," Tom said. "Do you understand?"

Oliver struggled for words—a unique experience for him. Usually he could be smooth under any circumstance, could sweet-talk anyone and everyone he came into contact with. It was all part of his CIA training. But this. . . this flat-out rejection from his only brother—his twin—was too much, even for him.

"Tom, I—"

"Stay away from my daughter, Oliver. Don't test me on this."

And with that, the line went dead. Oliver held the receiver against his face, unable to move. He hadn't expected Tom to jump up and down and do cartwheels over the phone call, but this completely disrespectful treatment was uncalled for. After everything he'd done to bring Tom home safely, to help his brother and his daughter, he certainly didn't deserve *this*.

With his hand shaking, Oliver slowly lowered the receiver onto the cradle. He took a steadying breath and lifted his drink again, downing the rest of it in one quick gulp.

It's going to be okay, he told himself, bracing his forearm with his other hand to stop the shaking. To stop the hot blood coursing through his veins from pushing him toward the edge—toward anger. *He'll come around eventually.*

But his thoughts were cold comfort to him, alone in his dark, unfurnished home. What did he have to do to get back in Tom's good graces? How many times would he have to prove himself?

AS THE SUN BEGAN TO SET OVER THE

By the Rules

city, and its red-gold light reflected off the mirrored façade of the more modern buildings, Gaia walked toward the front desk at Wallace and Wenk, the law offices that doubled as a front for the CIA's underground New York headquarters. Per Jake's advice, she was wearing the most responsible outfit she could piece together—her cleanest jeans topped by a light blue button-down shirt belonging to Jake that he hadn't worn since the ninth grade. Her hair was back in a bun, and she tried to walk with her chin up and her eyes straight ahead. The small, mousy woman behind the counter smiled tightly as Gaia approached.

"May I help you?" she asked.

"Yeah, I'm here to see Mr. Lawrence Vance," Gaia said, thrumming her fingers on the glossy marble countertop. The receptionist eyed her gnarled fingernails and Gaia clasped her hands behind her back.

"I see. And your name?" the woman asked dubiously.

"Gaia Moore. Please tell him I'm Tom Moore's daughter," Gaia said.

The receptionist hit a few buttons on the switchboard in front of her, then turned away from Gaia to speak into the receiver. This was never going to work—Gaia could feel it. It was Jake's idea to play by the rules—if she wanted to find out what was going on with Natasha and Tatiana, she would have to gain the respect and trust of the CIA. But Gaia didn't like it. She would have preferred to figure out a way to break in after dark and deal with things *her* way.

Of course, this was the CIA. Her way would probably get her shot dead on first sight.

"I'm to show you to one of our waiting rooms," the mousy woman said, seeming surprised as she hung up the phone. "Nancy, will you cover the phones for a sec?" she asked her counterpart. Then she led Gaia over to a bank of silver elevators at the back of the lobby. Once inside the sleek elevator, the woman stuck a key into a silver button, turned it, and depressed the button. The elevator moved swiftly down and Gaia almost lost her balance. She'd been expecting to be going up.

When the doors slid open again, a stern-looking woman, not much older than Gaia, stood in front of them in a gray suit and white blouse. She made an expression that may have passed for a smile in CIA circles.

"Ms. Moore. What a pleasure to meet you," she said, extending her hand. "I'm Agent Rosenberg."

Gaia shook the woman's hand and Agent Rosenberg looked at the receptionist. "You can go now, Jean. I'll take it from here."

"Later, Jean," Gaia said as the doors slid closed. Then she eyed Agent Rosenberg's skinny legs, her even skinnier arms, her sleek black hair. "You don't look like an agent," she said.

"Neither do you," Agent Rosenberg replied. "But I hear you can fight like one. Follow me."

Gaia did as she was told, keeping with the `play-by-the-rules plan`, but every cell in her body was jumping around: chaos. Natasha and Tatiana were here somewhere and it was all she could do to keep from laying the agent out and opening doors at random.

"In here, please," Agent Rosenberg said.

Gaia stepped inside a small office and Agent Rosenberg sat down at a silver table, looking up at Gaia expectantly. Gaia remained standing.

"Is Vance coming?" she asked.

"No. The director is otherwise occupied," Agent Rosenberg said. "What can I do for you?"

"They sent you to deal with me?" Gaia asked with a scoff. "You must be an intern or something like that."

"Actually I'm a special agent first class, and they wouldn't have sent me if they didn't want you to know that you're very important to this organization," Rosenberg said, her words clipped.

"But not important enough for the director," Gaia said.

"'Fraid not," Rosenberg replied, breaking diction temporarily. "Now, what can I do for you?"

Gaia stood across the room from Agent Rosenberg and crossed her arms over her chest.

"My dad was taken off the Petrova interrogation," Gaia said. "I want him back on."

"I'm sorry. We can't do that," Rosenberg said with a semblance of a smile.

"Then I want to interrogate them," Gaia said.

"I'm sorry. We can't do that," Rosenberg said.

"Why are you even bothering with me?" Gaia snapped.

"Why are you even bothering asking for things you know I can't give you?" Rosenberg replied, leaning forward. "You're a smart girl. Start asking the smart questions—the ones I might be able to help you with."

Gaia narrowed her focus, feeling as if she'd been reprimanded, but also feeling as if she'd been thrown a bone. She pulled over a metal chair and sat down, eyeing Agent Rosenberg, sizing her up.

"Can you tell me what they're saying in there?" Gaia asked finally.

"Not much," Agent Rosenberg replied.

"Have they given you any leads?" Gaia asked.

"Not yet," Agent Rosenberg said. But this time, there was a note of optimism in her tone. Gaia shifted in her seat.

"What's your plan to get them to talk?" she asked.

Agent Rosenberg smirked. "Now there's something I have been authorized to tell you. We've decided to split the prisoners up and offer them whichever bargaining chip would get them to talk. The only problem is, we're not entirely certain what that chip might be. We have a hunch, but we're not entirely certain."

There was a moment of silence as Gaia took this in. Agent Rosenberg gazed right into her eyes as if it were as easy as staring at a TV. Gaia felt a sudden moment of affinity with the woman. She seemed as close to fearless as any other human Gaia had come in contact with. She was all about control.

"You want my help," Gaia said.

Agent Rosenberg nodded. "Perceptive girl."

"What do I get?" Gaia asked.

"You get to help us find the person or persons who kidnapped your father," Rosenberg replied coolly. "And I will also keep you informed, as much as security clearance allows."

Gaia took a deep breath. It was better than nothing. "Okay, fine," she said. "Tell Tatiana that if she talks you'll let Natasha go and tell Natasha that if she talks you'll let Tatiana go."

"Interesting," Rosenberg said, nodding. "Offer the other prisoner's freedom, not her own."

"Trust me," Gaia said, feeling fairly satisfied with herself. "That's the only way to get to those two."

You know you're in trouble
when leaving messages becomes as
addictive as playing video games.
You're sitting in your room, and
you know you shouldn't start,
say, Super Collapse up again.
Your eyes are dry and your fingers are twitching and you're
definitely feeling the early
onset of carpal tunnel syndrome,
but you can't help yourself. You
keep thinking, *This is it. This
is the time I'm going to get to
the next level or beat my high
score*. And so you click it open
again, and you play, and you
almost never beat that high score
because now it's two A.M. and
you're dehydrated and dizzy and
you no longer know what the point
of the game is anyway.

But the whole leaving messages
thing is even worse. Because if you
play that video game until two
o'clock in the morning, the only
one that's going to know about it
is you. And even though you have a
headache the next morning and you

can see the little Collapse boxes
stacking up in your head when you
close your eyes, your shame is all
your own. There are no witnesses.
And you can live with your own
shame. You can delete the damn game
from your hard drive and move on.

But the messages are a different story because every time you
pick up the phone and dial, you
know somewhere in the back of
your mind that someone else is
going to hear whatever rambling
idiocy you're about to spew. You
know they're going to hear all
two, three, five, ten messages
and you know that no matter what
you say, all that's going to reg-
ister is, *"Hi, I'm a psycho and I
can't control myself."* And yet
you think you can fix it. You
think you can say just the right
thing to make all those other
messages disappear.

You're delusional. And this
time, you have witnesses.

Seeing
Oliver, she
was glad
she'd come.
Her uncle
looked
like

the

hermit

something
out of a
Charles
Dickens novel.

"YOU SHOULDN'T BE HERE," OLIVER

Donut Therapy

said the second he opened the door for Gaia on Saturday morning. His face was covered with patchy stubble and he looked as if he hadn't slept for more than five minutes the night before. His tired eyes were full of bitterness and sorrow.

"What's wrong?" Gaia asked, clutching her bag full of donuts and coffee.

Oliver didn't answer. He turned and walked back into the house, leaving the door only slightly ajar. To follow or not to follow, that was the question.

Gaia used the toe of her Doc Marten to push the door open and stepped out of the sunlight and into the dark depths of the brownstone. Oliver had kept the curtains drawn the whole time they were hiding out here, searching for clues on the whereabouts of her father, and it seemed her uncle hadn't let the sun in once since then. Didn't he know they were out of danger? Or had he just gotten used to the darkness?

"Gaia, I don't want to get you into trouble with your father," Oliver said wearily, lowering himself into a creaking chair at the one small, chipped table that stood against the far wall. There was a legal pad in front of him with a long list down the right side. Oliver capped the pen he'd obviously been using and pushed both things aside.

"If he knew you were here he would not be happy," he added.

Pretty depressing. *It looks like my donut therapy idea was long overdue,* Gaia thought. She'd woken up that morning and realized that Oliver might be hurting for company since Jake had left. She'd been up and out the door before her father had even stirred from his bedroom and now, seeing Oliver, she was glad she'd come. Her uncle looked like something out of a Charles Dickens novel.

"Tell me something I don't know," Gaia said with a smirk. "In case you hadn't noticed, I tend not to listen to authority."

Oliver smirked and nodded slowly as if he were sharing a private joke with himself.

Gaia placed the large waxed paper bag down on the table and started to unload the goods—a box of six fresh donuts and two huge cups of steaming coffee. She sat down across from Oliver and pulled her coffee over to her, popped the tab back, and inhaled the comforting scent. Oliver slid his own cup over the table and wrapped both hands around it. She noticed that his skin was dry to the point of cracking and that his fingers looked very pale.

Gaia swallowed hard and tried not to stare. After the mission in Russia she'd hoped that Oliver would start to come out of his shell a bit—start coming out of the brownstone every once in a while—but clearly he didn't feel he was ready for that yet. He was slowly turning into a hermit.

Maybe if Dad hadn't made him feel like the enemy, Gaia thought bitterly. *Maybe if he'd felt the least bit of warmth from his brother, he'd be feeling better about life.*

"Have you thought about. . . I don't know. . . getting some new furniture? A couple of lamps, maybe?" Gaia asked, looking around the depressing room. She was supposed to go shopping with her father that afternoon and wondered if she could sneak in a couple of purchases for her uncle. The man was going to go Unabomber if he didn't get a little light in this place. Maybe a painting or a poster to brighten things up.

Oliver's brows came together over his nose. "Hadn't really considered it."

Gaia's heart thumped. "Why not?" she asked. "I mean, you are going to stay here, right?" The last thing she wanted was for Oliver to skip town. Not now. Not before he made up with her father. She knew it was optimistic and probably very stupid of her, but she had this picture somewhere in the back of her mind— a picture of her and what was left of her family sitting down to dinner together, laughing and talking and just. . . being normal.

"I don't know, Gaia," Oliver said, his features softening a bit. "I think it might be better if I just. . . if I just disappeared."

"Why? Because that's what my father wants?" Gaia

asked, reddening. Oliver looked as if he'd been slapped. "I mean, because that's what you *think* my father wants?" she added. "He's just being him. He's just being. . . careful. He's going to come around eventually."

Oliver took a deep breath and leaned back. "I hope you're right," Oliver said. He placed his coffee cup down and slid the legal pad over so that it was resting in front of him again. He squinted down at the page, concentrating.

"What is that?" Gaia asked, grabbing a chocolate-covered donut and chomping into it. She used the back of her hand to wipe the crumbs from her mouth and leaned over to see the list as Oliver turned it toward her.

It was a list of names. And Sam Moon's was at the top.

"Okay," Gaia said, gazing at Oliver. "I still don't know what it is."

Oliver smiled slightly—sadly. "It's a list of people I need to make amends with," he explained. "I just started it, but I have a feeling it's going to get much, much longer."

Gaia looked down at the thirty or so names, her heart constricting. Oliver really was trying. He was trying so hard. And he was living out here by himself in Brooklyn like some kind of criminal banished from society. Why couldn't her father see how much he had changed?

Because he killed your mother. Because he tried to kill you on numerous occasions. Because he's evil, a little voice in Gaia's head told her.

But he wasn't evil. Not anymore. He was Oliver now, not Loki. And sooner or later her father was going to have to recognize that.

"Do you think Sam would talk to me?" Oliver asked, his eyebrows rising.

That question caught her completely off guard. She choked on her donut. "I don't know," Gaia replied truthfully. It was going to be a hard sell. Sam had lost several months of his life thanks to Loki. "But I'll see what I can do."

"That's all I can ask," Oliver replied, picking the list up again with two hands—almost reverently. When he looked up at Gaia once more, she could tell he was having one of his emotional moments. She concentrated to keep herself from squirming. She hated this part.

"Thank you for coming here, Gaia," Oliver said softly, his eyes moist around the edges. "It means a lot that you're still here for me."

"I know," Gaia said awkwardly. She reached up and pushed the bag of donuts toward him. "Eat something already."

Oliver smiled and picked up a jelly donut. Together they sat in companionable silence, until every last crumb was polished off.

TOM MOORE WALKED THROUGH THE

Decisions

Pottery Barn on 59th and Lexington, trying not to let his exhaustion and frustration show on his face. Like most men, he'd never been much of a shopper. He didn't have strong opinions about anything. Antique or modern, wood-finish or painted, steel or wrought iron. It was all the same to him. One would think that this blasé attitude would make this whole excursion easier—that he could pretty much just buy whatever he saw and be happy—but his lack of conviction just made him more irritated with himself.

He wanted to make a home with his daughter. And he hated that he didn't care what was in it. All he cared about was that it didn't look like it once belonged to Natasha.

"Dad? What about this bed?" Gaia asked from somewhere nearby.

Tom turned and saw Gaia standing next to a large, heavy, wooden bed with a high headboard. He was struck for the millionth time by how very much she looked like Katia—more and more each day. He smiled slightly, remembering how adorably frustrated his wife used to get whenever she took him out to the shops.

"Just make a decision, Tom!" she would say, *clutching two bedsheets in her delicate hands. "Plain white or blue stripes? Have an opinion!"*

"I like it," Tom said, walking over to Gaia and running his hand along the carvings at the top of the headboard. "This is the one."

Gaia smiled, clearly relieved that he'd finally picked something out. After five stores in all corners of the city, she had to be getting a bit tired. And while Gaia had quickly selected a new bed, desk, and linens at some of the independently owned stores downtown, the only thing Tom had so far was a lamp to replace the one he'd thrown at the wall in a fit of rage the day before. The truth was, the bed didn't inspire any great feelings within Tom, but the memory of Katia had. And he figured he might as well make this trip easier on their daughter like he was never able to for his wife.

Gaia walked over to a wall of shelves that held packages of sheets and pillowcases in brushed, brown silk.

"These look like they're you," Gaia said. "I mean, as much as sheets can *be* a person."

Tom smiled. "How so?"

Gaia considered, obviously choosing her words. She never would have admitted it, but Tom knew she was enjoying this shopping spree.

"They're manly man sheets," she said finally, blushing slightly. "Sophisticated, but—"

Tom reached out and ran his fingers over the smooth, velvety silk. "Sophisticated, but soft and mushy like your old man?" he joked, as he patted his less than solid stomach.

"Exactly," Gaia said with a laugh.

"Okay, so I'm a little more doughy than usual. . . . Next time I go to a Siberian prison, I'll have to remember my free weights." This made Gaia laugh even harder. Tom loved entertaining his daughter in this way.

Tom sat down on the bed and leaned back into the faux fur pillows, watching her as she searched for the right size. He took a deep breath and tried to calm the nerves that seemed to rear up every few minutes.

This was insane. He should be at headquarters right now, grilling Natasha. Deciphering what her cryptic clues about the past were all about. He should be trying to find out everything he could about his brother and the role he'd had in Tom's kidnapping. Instead he was kicking back in a superstore with fake fur bristles tickling the back of his neck.

"So, I went to see Oliver this morning," Gaia said suddenly, her back to him.

"What?" Tom blurted, bolting up. He felt all the blood rush to his head. "Gaia—"

"Dad, I think you should hear him out," Gaia said, tossing a set of sheets on the bed next to his bent leg.

"I am *not* going to hear him out and you are not going over there again!" Tom shouted, standing.

He looked at his daughter and his heart sank. She

suddenly seemed about four years old, standing there looking up at him with those wide, confused eyes. Tom glanced around the store and saw that a pair of older women and a younger couple had all frozen in place and were gaping at him. Tom felt his skin prickle with the heat of embarrassment.

"I'm sorry," he said quietly, coming around the bed. He ran his hand over Gaia's shoulder and down her arm, then squeezed her hand. "Gaia, I'm sorry," he repeated. "I'm just on edge. And when it comes to my brother. . ."

"I. . . I know," Gaia said, clearing her throat. "You don't have to explain." She moved away from him and made a big show of inspecting a set of old-fashioned clocks on a shelf at eye-level. Tom felt his chest empty out the moment she stepped away.

"But I do," Tom said, standing next to her. "For some reason I just haven't been able to control my emotions since we've been back," he told her. "But I'm working on it. I *am* sorry, Gaia."

"I know," Gaia said again. But this time she turned and looked him in the eye, attempting a smile.

"Listen, I know you care for your uncle, but I want you to trust me on this one," he told her. "I don't want you seeing him again until we know for sure that he had nothing to do with Natasha and Tatiana's attempts on your life. I don't trust him yet, Gaia. Just. . . humor me."

Gaia looked up into his eyes, her own wide and sure. "Okay, Dad," she said. "I won't see him again."

She was lying. She might not have even known it, but she was. Tom knew that Gaia would see Oliver again if she wanted to. She was an independent girl—always had been. And Tom had always admired it. Unfortunately it had also always scared him. Independence and fearlessness were not a good combination.

But as he looked into her eyes, he decided not to press the issue. Gaia had survived this long, mostly on her own. She was an intelligent, instinctive person, and Tom was proud of her. He was going to have to trust her to do what was right. Even if it meant swallowing his pride and keeping his mouth shut.

"Thank you," Tom replied. "Believe me, I want you to be right about this. You have no idea how much I want you to be right."

"I know," Gaia said, looking away. She lifted her hand toward the bed and let it slap down against her leg again. "So, you want to start loading up on this stuff so we can get out of here? I want to get home and see if they delivered *my* new stuff yet."

"Definitely," Tom said, feeling his head clear. "But I don't want any of that fur stuff," he added, finally making a real decision. "Not my style."

"I had a feeling," Gaia said with a smile.

She grabbed a basket and started to pick sheets and

shams and pillowcases off the shelf. Tom smiled wistfully as he watched her work. He promised himself there would be no more thinking about work and no more talking about Oliver for the rest of the day. All he wanted was to have a nice time with his daughter.

SAM STOOD OUTSIDE THE DOOR TO

Gaia's apartment and squared his shoulders. He tried to ready himself for whatever response she might give him. He had no idea what she was thinking after hearing all his messages—mainly because she'd never bothered to

The Gaia Loop

return them—but he had to find out. He had to know, once and for all, if what they had between them could still be salvaged.

The door swung open and Sam's heart skipped a few dozen beats. Gaia's face was flushed and her eyes were sparkling with something that could only be called happiness. Her hair was sticking out wildly around her face, having fallen loose from the ponytail that still held some of it back. She was wearing a white T-shirt and a pair of baggy jeans. When she reached up to smooth some hair behind her ear, the T-shirt rode up and exposed a tiny strip of her flat stomach.

"Sam," she said, the flush deepening. She crossed her arms over her chest and held herself. "Hi."

"Hey," Sam said. What was he supposed to say next? *Just wanted to see why you didn't return my calls.* Lame. He really should have thought this through.

"Gaia! Who is it?" a voice called from back in the living room. A man's voice.

Sam looked past Gaia into the apartment, where he could see basically nothing. "Bad timing?" he asked, his heart slamming into his rib cage.

"No!" Gaia said, finally stepping back. "Come in."

Sam followed Gaia past the kitchen and into the living room, which was littered with huge broken-down cardboard boxes, random pieces of oddly shaped Styrofoam, and enough bubble wrap to keep his fingers popping for days. Sam's eyes lit up when he saw Gaia's father stand up from behind a desk he was apparently assembling. At least, he hoped it was her father. The other option would have sent him running for the door.

"Sam Moon!" the man said brightly. He wiped his palm on the back of his jeans and held his hand out. "It's good to see you again."

"Mr. Moore," Sam said, shaking hands with the man. His grip was strong and his hands were calloused. "You're back."

"Thanks to Gaia," Mr. Moore said, smiling at his

daughter before returning to the manufacturer's directions he had laid out on the floor.

Sam turned to Gaia, a million questions in his mind. Last he heard, Gaia's father had disappeared from the hospital and she had no idea who had taken him or where, let alone why. Now the man was miraculously back home and building furniture in the living room like nothing had ever happened. A person could definitely miss *a lot* when they were out of the Gaia loop for a few short weeks.

A cold, hard ball formed around Sam's heart and he realized he was hurt. Hurt over being frozen out of Gaia's life. But he made himself remember that she *had* tried to apologize and it was he who pushed her away. He'd caused this.

"Oh, we just bought some new stuff," Gaia said, either misreading the question in his eyes or deciding to answer the easiest one first. "We're. . . redecorating."

"Cool," Sam said for lack of something better to say.

"So, what are you doing here?" Gaia asked, ever blunt.

"I . . . uh. . . was just hoping we could talk," Sam said quietly, moving toward the dining room table and away from her father. His shoved his hands into the pockets of his suede jacket and curled them into fists.

Gaia glanced in her dad's direction and Sam did the same. Clearly she sensed this was a conversation that couldn't take place with a parent around.

"Dad, I'm going to take a break," Gaia said, picking her jacket up off one of the dining room chairs. "I'll be back in a little while."

"Don't worry about me," her father said, his hand appearing from behind the back of the desk. "I'm sure I'll still be right here when you get back."

Gaia slipped into her battered army jacket and led the way out to the hall and the elevator. Sam could feel the tension between them as they stood side by side, watching the numbers light up as they descended to the lobby. He wished that he knew what she was thinking. He wished that he had a better handle on what *he* was thinking. All he knew was that his heart was racing and that he wanted this to go well.

The only question was: What did "well" mean? Did it mean that they would come out of this day as friends? Did it mean that they would come out of this day as a couple? Somewhere deep inside he knew that he wanted the latter, but would probably settle for the former.

His life was a lot less interesting without Gaia around—a lot less passionate and exciting and, yeah, dangerous, but still. . . . The occasional danger was a small price to pay for the other stuff.

Sam wanted back in the Gaia loop. He just hoped she was willing to let him in.

GAIA SAT DOWN ACROSS FROM SAM

at a back table at the Mikonos diner, wondering what the hell to say to break the excruciating silence. She wanted to apologize for not returning his calls. She wanted to ask him what had prompted them after he basically told her he never wanted to see her again. She wanted to know what he was thinking as he picked up the menu and pretended to look it over.

Twist

But every time she tried to formulate one of those questions in her mind it either came out sounding desperate, pathetic, or accusatory, none of which she actually felt.

"Oh, hey, Dmitri's back," Sam said, cutting into her thoughts. "He told me to tell you."

"Done laying low?" Gaia asked. "That's cool. I talked to him a couple of times on his cell, but I had no idea where he was."

"Yeah. He didn't even tell me," Sam said.

They fell back into awkward silence, each gazing out the window. Gaia was psyched by this new development. If Dmitri was back in town maybe he could help her track down her father's kidnapper. He had resources, contacts at the CIA. Between him and Rosenberg, maybe she could get somewhere.

She sighed and looked at the cow-spotted clock above the counter. If someone didn't say something soon she was going to have to bail. Of course, there was *one* thing she *had* to talk to Sam about and now was as good a time as any. Gaia took a sip from the water glass that the busboy had slapped down on the table and cut right to the chase.

"My uncle wants to meet with you," she said.

Sam dropped the menu down flat on the table. "You're kidding me."

"No. I know it's a lot to ask, but—"

"A lot to ask? Gaia, the guy kept me in an eight-by-eight cell for six months! Why the hell would I want to meet with him?" Sam blurted.

"But it wasn't him," Gaia told him. "You know that. He only wants to meet with you because he wants to apologize for what Loki did."

Sam lifted his hand and rubbed at his forehead with his thumb and forefinger. He pressed his eyes closed and took a steadying breath. "I don't want to talk about this right now," he said finally.

Gaia heard the pain in his voice and the effort Sam was making to control it. She decided to drop the subject—for now. She'd broached it and now he could have some time to think it over.

"Fine," she said as the waitress approached. Gaia ordered a Coke and a plate of cheese fries, and Sam asked for a black coffee.

"So. . . ," he said as the waitress scurried away.

"So," she replied. She was going to let him bring it up, whatever it was. He was the one who had called her. He was the one who had come over. She wasn't going to say a word until he told her what he was thinking. It was a convenient decision to make since she had no idea what to think herself.

"So, your dad's back," Sam said, pushing his water glass back and forth between his hands. "That's amazing."

Gaia blinked. "Yeah. My uncle and I tracked him down, actually," she said. Instantly her thoughts turned to Jake and his role in rescuing her father. Should she tell Sam about him? And if so, what should she tell? The whole Jake thing was so complicated in her mind, she wasn't sure she could explain it to herself, let alone to Sam.

She also knew that whatever Sam was thinking, there was a chance he might shut down if she mentioned another guy. Even if she and Sam were no longer together, she knew that he would assume that she and Jake were more than friends if he knew what Jake had done for her. And if he thought they were more than friends, uncomfortableness would ensue. That was the last thing Gaia wanted.

"Where was he?" Sam asked, leaning back as the waitress placed their orders in front of them. "I mean, unless it's top secret."

"He was in Russia," Gaia replied. "We're still not sure who took him."

She shoved a few fries in her mouth and they

settled in her stomach like sticks. *We're still not sure who took him,* the words repeated in her mind. Maybe she shouldn't have left her father alone.

"Hey, it's okay," Sam said suddenly, reading her expression. "He's home now. You guys are going to be okay."

Gaia watched as Sam's hand slowly came down on top of her own. The warmth of his skin sent a shiver up her arm and she didn't pull away. It was amazing how comforting one touch could be. She had thought Sam was never going to touch her again.

"I know," she said.

His fingers closed a little more tightly around her palm and Gaia felt a jolt of something—something unpleasant. Something that felt a whole lot like guilt.

Jake, she thought, her stomach churning. *I feel guilty because of Jake.*

She swallowed hard and stared at Sam's hand on her own. This was a new and unexpected twist. She knew that she was attracted to Jake. She knew that he had pretty much become her best friend. But guilt over holding hands with another guy? How had it come to this?

You have to tell Sam, Gaia's inner voice told her. *Pull your hand away. Tell him it's over.*

But she couldn't. Sam held a huge part of Gaia's heart and he was finally here. He clearly cared about her and wanted to be part of her life. If she said anything now, that would all be obliterated. She wasn't ready to let go of him yet.

"What're you thinking?" Sam asked.

Tell him about Jake! Say something!

"Nothing," Gaia replied, removing her hand and picking up another fry. "I wasn't thinking about anything."

As she shoveled a few cheesy fries into her mouth, she decided that, for now, Jake was going to remain on the back burner. For now, she just wanted to be with Sam. She owed it to him, and to herself, to see if they could be friends again.

She could deal with her intense emotional confusion later.

I'm no good at this stuff. Never have been. Probably never will be. I suck at figuring out how people feel about me. But I suck even more at figuring out how I feel about them. It took me forever to figure out that the nausea I always felt around Sam was attraction. It took me even longer to realize that I was in love with Ed. But in both those cases, there were a million other factors to complicate things. There was Heather, for example. And there was the fact that being with anyone put that person in immediate danger. Sam was kidnapped because of me. Ed was almost killed. It made it kind of hard to even think about being close to someone.

But now. . . now things have changed. It's really as simple as that when you get down to it. There's nothing to protect Jake from. And even if there was, he's not a person who would tolerate being protected. He's made that more than clear. So now I have to deal. I have to deal with the fact that, yeah, I'm attracted to him. There, I said it. I have to deal with the fact that when I was with Sam today, I couldn't stop thinking about Jake. I have to deal with the fact that I look forward to seeing him. That when I'm with him my thoughts are mostly positive. That whenever we happen to touch or brush up against each other, I get that shiver all over my skin.

I have to deal. I have to figure out how I feel. Because there aren't any more excuses not to.

To: X22
From: Y
Subject: RE: Prisoner 352, Codename Abel

Receipt of message confirmed. Send all NYC units into the field. I want daily reports on the movements of Genesis, Cain, and Abel. Don't fail me on this.

Could she
really do
this? Could
she really
just take
off on the
spur of the
moment and
go have fun?

time

to

try

"GAIA! WHAT A PLEASANT SURPRISE!"

Touched

Dmitri held the door to his Murray Hill apartment open for Gaia on Saturday morning and she smiled as she walked by. She may have been there on business, but she had a soft place in her heart for the kindly old man who had helped her bring Natasha to justice. It was good to see him again.

"How have you been?" Dmitri asked, settling into a cushy leather chair in his plush living room. Gaia sat across from him on the couch and leaned forward.

"Okay," she said. "But I need your help."

"What is it?" Dmitri asked, his expression growing concerned.

"The CIA put my father on forced leave and they won't let either one of us near Natasha and Tatiana," Gaia said in a rush. "Which means we're nowhere on the investigation into my father's kidnapping."

Dmitri nodded slowly, taking this in. "Why did they put your father on leave?"

"I don't know," Gaia said, standing up and starting to pace. "He won't tell me and neither will they."

"You talked to someone at the CIA?" Dmitri asked, raising his eyebrows. He brought his fingertips together under his nose in a contemplative pose as he watched her circle in front of him.

"Yeah, some special agent," Gaia said. "She's going

to grill Natasha and Tatiana separately. I told her what to dangle in front of them to make them talk, but who knows if it'll work. . . ."

Dmitri shifted in his seat and brought his hands together under his nose. "What did you tell her to do?"

Gaia really looked at him for the first time since the conversation started. There was a new tension in his voice. He was legitimately apprehensive. Gaia was touched.

"I told her to offer Natasha Tatiana's freedom and vice versa," she said with a shrug.

Dmitri narrowed his eyes and nodded, then took a deep breath. "Yes. Very wise," he said, now gazing off across the room. "That just might do the trick."

"Anyway, do you think there's anything you can do?" Gaia asked, sitting down on the edge of the couch again. "Can you call your guy at the CIA and see what he knows? Or. . . I don't know, use some of your other contacts—find out if they've gotten any rumblings out of Russia? Maybe people are talking about the rescue. . . ."

Dmitri sat in silence for a moment, eyeing her, mulling over everything she'd told him. Finally he sat up and leaned forward, resting his forearms on his knees. His face moved into the shaft of light coming from a nearby lamp, illuminating every last line and wrinkle in his weathered face.

"Gaia, I know you're not going to like this, but I think it's time for you to let this go," he said.

Gaia felt as if he'd just punched her right in the gut. With brass knuckles. "What? Let what go? The fact that Natasha and Tatiana betrayed us? The fact that someone kidnapped my father? What if they try it again?"

"They won't try it again," Dmitri said, his blue eyes sure. "Trust me."

"How can you know that?" Gaia demanded.

"You've already proven that you won't be intimidated—that you won't respond to their tactics," Dmitri said. "Believe me, Gaia. I know how these people work."

Gaia couldn't comprehend what she was hearing. She had been so sure that Dmitri would help her. So confident that he was her best ally in this. Why was he turning her down?

"Please, Gaia. It's time to move on," Dmitri said, reaching for her hands. "Let it go and live your life. Let the CIA do its job."

Gaia scoffed and stood again, pulling her hands from his. "You sound just like my father."

Dmitri chuckled and looked up at her. "I suppose I should take that as a compliment."

"Whatever," Gaia said, turning her back on him and heading for the door.

"Gaia! I want you to know that whatever happens, I will always be here for you!" Dmitri called after her.

Gaia paused for only a second, then kept walking,

wondering why she had hesitated at all. Why those words had for some reason touched a chord within her heart.

"Yeah," she said under her breath. "Thanks for nothing."

TOM WALKED TOWARD CENTRAL PARK, his arms crossed over his chest, his eyes trained on the ground. He took a few long, deep breaths of the fresh spring air and felt the soothing warmth of the **Let Go** sun wash over him. Once he'd finished putting together Gaia's new furniture that morning, he'd found himself slowly going stir-crazy. His new bed and dresser were going to be delivered later in the week and he still couldn't seem to make himself comfortable among Natasha's things. He felt more stifled in that apartment with her books and her knickknacks and her scent than he had in any prison cell he'd ever had to call home.

Who was she working for? Tom wondered for the ten billionth time since he'd learned that Natasha was, in fact, the enemy. *She had to be working for someone. Who was it? The Russian Mafia? The Russian Secret Service? One of the newer spy organizations?*

He entered the park and passed by a few empty benches, not ready to sit yet. He had too much pent-up energy to expend. He'd walk the whole way to the other side and back if he had to. Whatever it took for him to figure this out.

Of course, the problem was, he was fairly certain he already had it figured out. As much as Gaia wanted to believe otherwise, Tom knew that Loki had to have been the one pulling the strings. It was the only scenario that made sense. No one had questioned him while he was in Russia. No one had tortured him or demanded he divulge his secrets. There didn't seem to be any point to him being there other than to keep him from being here. Who would go to all those lengths to remove him from his daughter other than Loki?

"Damn it," Tom said through his teeth. He stuffed his hands under his arms and clamped his elbows down, coiling in on himself. *How had Loki done it? That was what he wanted to know. How had he faked a coma? How had he given orders from a hospital room? How had he convinced Gaia that he was Oliver again?*

I need to talk to Natasha. She's the only one who knows, Tom thought, trying not to notice the mother who was pulling her toddler to her as he passed by, clearly disturbed by his whacked-out demeanor. *How could I have been so stupid? How could I have let her get to me?*

The answer, he knew, was simple. He let her get to him because he was in love with her. And her betrayal stung more than anything he'd suffered in the past. She'd fooled him into opening a heart that had been closed for a decade, and then she'd turned on him. If he was ever going to figure out what was going on with her and her daughter and Loki, he was going to have to get past that.

Tom paused at a fork in the paved pathway. He forced himself to uncurl his arms. Forced himself to look up at the oncoming dusk. He breathed in and out, expanding his chest and closing his eyes. He breathed in and out and told himself to let go. He had to. For his daughter. For his own sanity.

When he opened his eyes again, he looked at the two paths that lay ahead. One wound up and into the budding bushes and trees, the other was straight and sloped down toward the center of the park. Tom turned right and took the easier path. He wanted to stroll. He wanted to relax. It was time to let go.

He'd only taken a few long strides when the trill of his cell phone surprised him. He pulled it out of his pocket and flipped it open in one smooth motion.

"Moore here," he said into the mouthpiece.

"Agent Moore, it's Director Vance. There's been a development."

Tom blinked and stepped off the pathway to let a pair of skateboarders pass. "What kind of development?" he asked, his pulse beginning to race.

"We need you to come in," the deep, throaty voice replied. "Now."

66

"What about taking some time off?" Tom said, unabashedly enjoying this. They needed him. He knew they needed him.

"I'm ending it," Vance replied firmly. "I expect to see you in fifteen."

GAIA SAT ON THE COUCH ON SATURDAY

Used Undies

evening, brooding over her meeting with Dmitri. For the last hour she'd been alternating between obsessive irritation and obsessive brainstorming—trying to think of other ways to help her dad. He'd left her a message saying he was going back to work, which was good, but that didn't mean they were putting him back on the case. He might still need her, and even if he didn't, there was no way to stop her mind from obsessing.

When the doorbell rang, however, her thoughts came to a screeching stop. She jumped up, crossed the living room, and slipped the cover on the peephole aside.

Jake, she thought, her heart responding with the usual thump, much to her chagrin.

"I know you're there. I heard the peephole thing move," Jake said.

Gaia rolled her eyes and opened the door. Jake looked even more perfect in full, undistorted size than he had through the peephole. He was wearing black pants and shoes and a formfitting burgundy T-shirt that made his olive skin look even darker. His black leather jacket was new—at least she hadn't seen it before—and his hair was slightly gelled.

"Why are you dressed like that?" Gaia asked, stepping aside so that he could come in.

"It's Saturday night," Jake replied, opening his hands. "I think the more appropriate question is why are *you* dressed like *that?*"

Gaia flushed and crossed her arms over her chest. After she had returned from Dmitri's that afternoon, she'd taken a shower and braided her still-wet hair down her back. Then she'd slipped into her most comfortable cargo pants, a black T-shirt, and a black hooded sweatshirt for her night on the couch. What did Jake expect her to do, lounge around in silk and cashmere?

"So, you came here to insult my wardrobe?" Gaia asked.

"You started it," Jake said. He clapped his hands together and grinned. "Actually, I came here to take you out. Whatever you want to do, wherever you want to go."

Gaia blinked and drew herself up straight. Wait. Had he just asked her out? Where was the awkwardness? The agonizing silence? How was she supposed to have the time to get all mortified and embarrassed and confused if he just sprung it on her like that?

"I. . . uh. . ."

Okay, there it was. `Total loss of communication skills.` This felt more familiar.

"Come on, what do you do for fun?" Jake asked, his high energy bursting out of him and ricocheting off the walls. Gaia had a mental vision of herself ducking and dodging to avoid being hit by a shot of Jake oomph.

"What do I do for fun. . . ?" Gaia repeated, stalling.

This is pathetic, she thought, racking her brain. *I don't have an answer to that question.* But when had she ever had the chance to think about it? When had she ever been misery-free long enough to even consider having fun? Yeah, she'd had a few laughs with Ed, but she couldn't exactly tell Jake that she hung out with Ed for fun. Besides, hanging out with him was not an option. Not anymore.

"Um. . . chess?" Gaia said finally, pathetically.

Jake, understandably, laughed. "You have to be kidding me," he said, walking over and standing across from her. "You live in one of the most kickass cities in the world. There are a million things to do here and you pick chess."

"It's. . . challenging," Gaia said, defeated. She let her shoulders slump and looked up into his eyes. She felt like the biggest geek in the world, standing in front of some popular, fun-loving guru and begging him to help her become functional in society.

"Okay, you need help," Jake said, as if reading her mind.

He abruptly turned left and walked down the hall toward her bedroom. Gaia followed, somehow resisting the urge to tackle him to the floor before he got there. Her room was a constant mess, with tangles of clothes, cupcake wrappers, soda cans, and who knew what else littering the floor. If he went in there, he was sure to get a glimpse of something embarrassing, like socks with holes in them or bras with fraying straps or worst of all, used undies.

Please don't let him see any used underwear, Gaia thought, squeezing her eyes shut as she entered the room.

But Jake didn't even look around. He went straight to her closet and pulled out a slim-fitting black turtleneck. He tossed it at her and then started going through a pile of jeans—Tatiana's jeans.

"I'm *not* wearing her clothes," Gaia said. She grabbed a pair of white cotton panties off the floor and stuffed it under her new pillows.

"Understood," Jake replied, turning to her side of the closet again. "Do you own anything that isn't army green?"

Gaia flushed. Why had he come over here? To remind her of how unappealing she was? To show her that she didn't even own one single piece of clothing that a guy would find attractive? Jake was turning out to have some serious nerve.

"You know. . . ," Gaia began, but she never got to finish. Jake gave up on the closet and stepped so close to Gaia her nose was practically pressed into his chest. He reached around behind her and she felt a tug at the bottom of her braid. She held her breath as she felt his fingers running through her hair, fanning it out over her shoulders.

Jake pulled back and looked down at her, smiling almost gently. "Wear whatever you want," he said. "But I am taking you out of here."

Then he turned and walked out of the room, closing the door behind him. Still struggling to breathe, Gaia stepped in front of the full-length mirror that Tatiana had secured to the back of their door. Her hair was dry now and the haphazard braid had woven it in hundreds of loose waves. Gaia ran her fingers through it, trying to see whatever it was that had made Jake smile like that. She pulled it all over one shoulder and turned to the side.

Street rat, she thought.

"You coming?" Jake called out.

And right in front of her own reflection, Gaia smiled. Instantly. Purely. Without thinking about it. It was so odd, this actual spontaneous emotion. Could she really do this? Could she really just take off on the spur of the moment, forgo a night of obsessing and just have fun?

As she stood there, staring at herself, Gaia realized that she wanted to try.

She ripped off her sweatshirt and tee, pulled on the turtleneck, and yanked her hair out of the collar. Then she grabbed her denim jacket and her messenger bag and strode out of her room.

It was time to see what this fun thing was all about.

Getting There

"THANKS, MAN. I OWE YOU ONE," Jake said, slapping hands with his friend Derek Simms at the entrance to section 79 at Madison Square Garden.

Derek worked as a security guard at the Garden and had just smuggled Jake and Gaia in through a back entrance. The Knicks were playing a crappy team, so there were empty seats all over the arena and Derek was giving them two of the best.

"Yeah, when are you going to get a job *I* can take advantage of?" Derek asked, laughing as he gripped Jake's hand.

"We'll see," Jake said. They slapped each other's backs and then Derek loped off to return to his post.

Jake looked around and found Gaia standing at the top of the stairs, watching the action on the court. Her hair looked so touchable with all those waves, its million shades of blond shifting every time she moved. He could still feel its softness under his fingertips.

Get a grip, man, Jake told himself, rolling his shoulders back. Gaia was definitely a closed book and he knew it was going to take a lot of patience before he got to touch that hair again. He should count himself lucky that she didn't knee him in the groin the first time.

"Pretty sick, huh?" he asked, stepping up next to Gaia. Even with an undercapacity crowd, the place seemed to be filled with screaming fans in blue and orange. The butter-colored boards of the court gleamed under the bright lights and the loudspeaker blared a cavalry horn recording, prompting everyone in the arena to shout, "Charge!"

"I've never been to a game here," Gaia said, her eyes trained on Allan Houston as he drove down the court.

"Never? Well then, you'll need to have the full experience," Jake said. "I'll meet you at the seats."

"Where are you going?" Gaia asked, her blue eyes wide.

"Trust me," Jake said with a grin.

He waited until Gaia had settled into one of the seats Derek had pointed out, then turned and jogged over to the nearest souvenir stand. He picked out a blue-and-orange Knicks visor, a white tank top with a small logo on the chest, two huge foam fingers, and a tan fisherman-style cap for himself. The girl behind the counter eyed him like he was a crazy person as she handed over the goods and took a major wad of his cash. Then Jake hit the food counter and bought a couple of hot dogs and sodas. Balancing everything in his arms on the way back down the stairs, Jake thanked God that he had an aisle seat. Anyone he had to walk over would have killed him.

"What is all that?" Gaia asked as everyone around them stood up and cheered a killer three-point shot.

Jake placed the food tray down on his empty seat and handed the tank top, the visor, and the foam finger to Gaia, one by one.

"I'm not putting this stuff on," Gaia said flatly.

"Live a little, G," Jake told her, pulling the fisherman's cap down over his own eyes. He knew he probably looked like a tool, but that was the point. Gaia was going to have fun tonight if it killed him. Even if he had to embarrass the hell out of himself to make it happen.

He slipped the other foam finger on over his hand and raised it in the air. "Go, Knicks!" he shouted, tipping his head back. The fans all around him let out a huge cheer.

Gaia laughed and shook her head, her eyes dancing. Jake's heart flipped over. She'd laughed. He wasn't sure if he'd ever seen that before. Suddenly Gaia cleared her throat and looked away, flushing as if she'd done something wrong. Was it possible that she had actually never laughed before? Okay, probably not. But she obviously didn't do it much.

"Just put the tank top on over your shirt," he told her.

"What is it with you and dressing me?" Gaia asked. "Do you miss your Barbie dolls?"

Jake tucked his chin and looked up at her past the brim of his hat. "Put it on or you don't get the hot dog."

Gaia sighed and tilted her head so she could see the foot-long waiting for her in the cardboard tray. He could tell she was caving.

"Fine," she said finally. She took off her jacket, pulled the shirt on over her turtleneck, then slipped her jacket back on. While she was still adjusting herself, Jake placed the visor on her head and put the foam finger in her lap. Gaia rolled her eyes up and looked at the visor, then shook her head again, trying not to smile. She yanked the foam finger on and looked at Jake expectantly.

"Hot dog," she said, holding out her free hand.

Jake finally sat down, lifting the tray onto his lap, and handed her the goods. Gaia consumed a third of the hot dog in one huge bite.

"I'm good now," she said, chewing. And she actually did look good. She looked comfortable... content. And ridiculously cute. She lifted her foam finger to shoulder level. "Go, Knicks," she said quietly.

Jake smiled and bit into his own hot dog. "You're getting there."

TOM STOOD IN ONE OF THE DEBRIEF-

ing rooms at the CIA's New York headquarters, completely calm and composed. He'd changed into a clean, starched suit and a tie and made sure there was no stray stubble on his face, no hair out of place on his head. Whatever he'd been called in to do, he was going to do it. He was going to prove that he was back on his game.

Get It Done

The door opened noiselessly and Director Vance entered the room, followed by two other agents—a young woman Tom had met two days ago named Clarissa Rosenberg, who was a behavioral specialist, and Trey Frenz, an agent Tom had trained with as a neophyte whom he'd never much liked. Tom ignored the presence of the other two and trained his eyes on Vance.

"Agent Moore, we've cut your leave of absence short—"

"Very short," Tom couldn't resist saying. Vance ignored his joke.

"Because since you left on Thursday afternoon, the prisoners have refused to speak to anyone," Vance continued.

Tom blinked. "What does that have to do with me?"

"They've refused to speak to anyone. . . but *you*," Vance said, averting his gaze for a split second. Tom felt a twitch on his lips and forced it away. He was not going to smile. He was not going to rub his triumph in his director's face. Vance was not the type of man who would find it amusing.

"We even took your daughter's advice, Agent Moore, offering each the other's freedom, but they didn't bite," Agent Rosenberg said. "At least not until now."

"Wait a second—Gaia was here?" Tom asked, baffled.

"She didn't tell you?" Agent Rosenberg asked.

"No," Tom said, making a mental note to ask a few questions of Gaia later. Now was no time to dwell on daughterly missteps. "Which one of them gave in? Which one is ready to talk?"

"Natasha," Agent Rosenberg said. "Call it a motherly instinct."

"So you're going back in there," Vance said. "Agent Rosenberg will be monitoring the prisoners' behavior, looking for body language, expressions, anything to indicate subterfuge."

"I'm sure I can—"

"I just want a second eye," Vance said. "These women know how to beat a lie detector but no one has ever snowed Agent Rosenberg."

The woman smiled slightly at the compliment, then quickly rearranged her sharp features.

"He's right. Your reputation precedes you," Tom told her.

"Thank you, Agent Moore," she said, a slight blush working its way across her high cheekbones.

"Agent Frenz is here to keep an eye on you, when I'm not in the observation area, and make sure you don't screw up again," Vance continued. Frenz smirked and Tom didn't give him the satisfaction of noticing.

"Agent Moore, I don't think I have to remind you of how delicate a situation this is," Director Vance said, stepping so close to Tom he could smell what the man had eaten for dinner. "Do you think you're ready for this?"

"I am, sir," Tom said, filled with conviction.

He did an internal systems check and was relieved to find that he was telling the truth. His pulse was slow, his body temperature normal. He didn't feel in the least bit stressed or excited or angry. All he wanted was to get it done.

"In fact, I'm quite looking forward to hearing what the prisoner has to say. . . ."

I've dated girls with secrets before, but Gaia is a completely new kind of cagey. I thought after the whole Tatiana shoot-out, after playing Triple X in Russia, after fighting for our lives together with her crazy father and uncle, after telling me about her mother's death that there couldn't possibly be anything else she was keeping from me.

But there's more. I know it. There's something else. Something else big. Something that's keeping her from trusting me completely. I can tell in the way she's always darting her eyes around when I ask questions. And sometimes I feel like she's on the verge of saying some-thing and then she stops herself. I mean, what is it? She's pretty much with me most of the time.

Could her family have even more deep dark dramas that she doesn't want to reveal? Is that even pos-sible? Is it something about her mom, maybe—or the reason her dad and uncle, like, hate each other?

Is it secret worthy? Something more than your standard dysfunctional spy-family crap?

I've got to admit, it scares me just a little bit. I mean, what could be bigger than the fact that her family is full of spies and that she's constantly a target? If there's something bigger than *that*, it's got to be a little scary.

The thing is, it's not scary enough to keep me away. It's not scary enough to even make a dent in the attraction I feel toward her. I've never felt anything like this before. And it's not just that she's hot. I mean, she *is*, but it's not just that. It's something else. There's just something about her. Something that makes me think about her all the time and crave her when I'm not around her.

So whatever that secret is, it's not going to scare me away. And sooner or later, she's going to tell me what it is. Because, unless I am totally off base, I think she's starting to feel the same way about me.

What had made
her think that
she could get
away with one
normal, fun
night? **trapped**
Didn't she know
the fates were
working against
her here?

GAIA WAS IN SUGAR HEAVEN. SHE
had passed Dylan's Candy Bar a
hundred times since its grand
opening, but had never stopped
in, and now that she was there,
she felt as if she'd come home,
made peace with the universe.
This place was built for her.

Freelance Vigilante Work

"I can't believe you've never
been in here," Jake said, watching as Gaia selected a huge bag
of Gummi Bears to add to her basket. "You live less
than ten blocks away."

"I know. I have issues," Gaia said. But now that she'd
been inside, she knew she was definitely coming back.
Possibly on a daily basis. The two-story candy shop had
every sugar-fix item Gaia had ever loved plus dozens of
things she'd never even heard of. They had Wonka Bars,
M&M's in every color in a Crayola box, and an ice
cream counter with flavors only dreamed of in heaven.

Maybe I should get a job here, she thought, imagin-
ing the damage she could do with an employee discount.

"So, I tell you we can go anywhere in the city and
you drag me all the way back up and across town to go
to a place, like, ten blocks from your house," Jake said,
gnawing on a piece of black licorice.

"You said it was my choice," Gaia pointed out.

"Just wanted to be sure we're clear," Jake said, smiling. He looked down at her overflowing basket and frowned. "You're going to be on a sugar high for the rest of the year."

"Pretty much," Gaia said.

She took one last pass by the novelty wall, grabbed another Spider-Man pop, and deposited her basket on the counter. As the girl started to ring up her purchases, Jake pulled out his wallet. Gaia grabbed his wrist and pushed it back down under the counter.

"I got it," she said, the words "sugar daddy" ironically popping into her head. Every time Jake paid for something—cotton candy at the Knicks game, the cab to get back uptown—she felt more and more like this was a date. And the more she felt like it was a date, the more self-conscious she became. Gaia and dates did not mix.

Besides, she couldn't be out on a *date* while her father was interrogating Natasha and Tatiana. She couldn't be out on a date while her dad's kidnapper was still out there somewhere. It was just wrong.

Better for her subconscious to think she was just hanging out, even if on some level she was hoping this was a date, and Jake seemed to be hoping that, too. Her subconscious, after all, was the entity that made her say stupid things, drop entire plates of food in her own lap, and automatically punch the lights out of anyone who touched her.

The total for the candy was astronomical, but Gaia barely even blinked. It was worth it just for the experience. Jake held the door open for her as she maneuvered her way outside while simultaneously ripping open a bag of chocolate-covered pretzels. She bit into one and closed her eyes, savoring the taste. This had to be what happiness felt like.

"So, you up for more or do you want to head home?" Jake asked. "Cuz there's this band playing at CB's Gallery tonight. This guy Shiva from my dojo said he's seen them play. They're supposed to be pretty good."

Jake pulled a wrinkled fluorescent green flyer out of his pocket and showed it to Gaia. The ad was for a band called the Dust Magnets, and there was a scraggly line drawing of an angry-looking dust-bunny playing the guitar. The illustration looked vaguely familiar, but Gaia couldn't place it.

"Where'd you get this?" she asked, turning the page over.

"They were plastered all over Oliver's neighborhood," Jake said with a shrug. "I tore it down the other day and figured I'd check it out if I was around."

Gaia popped another pretzel into her mouth and considered the invitation. She was hardly ever home at a reasonable hour, but that was usually because she was on the lam or kicking someone's ass. But her many months of living the street urchin lifestyle had turned her into a serious night person. She wasn't remotely tired, and if she went home she was just going to sit there and obsess until her father called. Besides, now she had supplies. With the amount of food in her bag, she could go all night.

"Why not?" she said, stepping off the curb and heading for the subway. It might be cool to stay out just for fun instead of staying out to find free-lance vigilante work.

As long as it wasn't a date.

The Kicker

ED SAT BACK INTO THE CUSHY COUCH he'd managed to secure at CB's Gallery by arriving there at the very uncool hour of eight o'clock. He'd been sitting there on and off ever since, only getting up when Kai or one of her friends was there to save the seat. He figured if he was going to have to listen to Kai's brother's punk band destroy the honor and legacy of punk bands everywhere, he may as well do it from a comfortable couch.

"Hey there!" Kai said, returning from the stage where she'd been chatting with the band's drummer for the last fifteen minutes while he set up. Between the bright graphic tank top she was wearing and the glitter swept onto strategic portions of her face and shoulders, Kai was absolutely glowing. All day and all evening, Kai had been even more hyper than usual, running around, thanking everyone from school for coming. Over the past week she'd been putting up flyers advertising the gig on bulletin boards, windows, and every other empty surface she could find at the Village School.

"Miss me?" she asked, plopping down next to him.

"Yeah, totally," Ed replied, forcing a smile.

He wasn't exactly sure how to act around Kai these days. Ever since she'd basically offered her body up to him and he'd frozen faster than a shallow puddle on an Antarctic night, being with her made him tense. He was always worried she was going to try it again and he was going to bail again and she was going to start thinking he was gay. Or just really lame.

Not that she was going to undress in the middle of a crowded club, but sooner or later he was going to have to deal with the after-the-club situation.

To top it all off, it seemed that every last member of her brother's band, the Dust Magnets—minus her own brother, of course—was in love with Kai. They'd all been shamelessly flirting with her for the past hour, buying her drinks, making her laugh. And the kicker was, it didn't bother Ed in the slightest. He wasn't jealous. He wasn't proprietary. He wasn't anything.

Kai was a cool girl, but there was just no sparkage.

"Okay, you have contemplative face," Kai said, touching her fingertip to the top of his nose, which was wrinkled in concentration. "What's wrong?" She'd curled her black hair into a million perfect tendrils and they bounced around her face as she shifted in her seat, resting her elbow on top of his shoulder.

"Nothing," Ed replied. "Just can't wait for the music to start."

Kai's face lit up. "I know! Steve is so excited! They're totally pumping up the amps. They're going to bring this place to its knees!"

Yeah. Wailing in pain, Ed thought.

He looked at the door as he had been every time it opened, not knowing whom he expected to see, but hoping it was somebody, anybody, with whom he could share his pain. This time none other than Sam Moon walked in, followed by a horde of friends. He looked around and almost immediately spotted Ed.

Sam lifted his chin and Ed did the same, acknowledging his former nemesis in the battle for Gaia Moore's heart. Then he looked away. He knew Sam wasn't going to make pleasantries and neither was he. But seeing the guy did make Ed wonder.

What was Gaia doing tonight? And wherever she was, was she half as bored as him?

SAM GRIPPED FOUR BOTTLES OF beer between his fingers as he carefully wove his way around tables and chairs and feet— not to mention the dozens of bags and backpacks that had been stowed on the floor. His roommate, Aidan, had found a

The Chick Stare

table up near the stage with their other friends, the better to support Johnny Chen, the drummer of the band who had not only wheedled all of them into coming, but also into wallpapering their entire neighborhood in Brooklyn with those hideous green flyers. Johnny was Aidan's former roommate at NYU. They'd lived together as freshmen, hated each other as sophomores, and now that they were living in separate boroughs and hardly ever saw each other, they were best friends.

There was a whole long story involving a girl they'd fought over and a fishing trip in which they'd gotten marooned at sea, but Sam had never quite followed it. All he knew was, Aidan and Johnny were now friends and that was why he was here.

Why Ed Fargo was here was an entirely different question. Sometimes New York was entirely too small for comfort.

"Thanks, man," Aidan said as Sam placed the bottles down in the center of the imbalanced table. "What do we owe you?"

"Forget it. We'll settle up later," Sam said. He leaned his shoulder blades into the cane-backed chair and heard an ominous crack, so he sat forward again. His friends had left him a seat facing the stage, so he had to crane his neck all the way around to see Ed. Which, for some reason, was very important to him.

Because you want to see if Gaia's going to show, Sam admitted to himself. Over the past year he'd grown accustomed to admitting these things to himself.

He took a slug of his beer, then hunched his shoulders, elbows propped on the table. He turned his head slightly, making like he was just checking out the door. Ed was still sitting on the same couch with some pretty Asian girl practically straddling him. Sam smiled and turned around again.

Apparently Gaia wouldn't be making an appearance.

"So, I heard this band rocks," Jeff Miller said, already sucking the dregs from the bottom of his bottle.

"Yeah? I heard they suck," Aidan replied.

"Then why'd you make us come here?" Charlie asked.

At that moment, Johnny came down from the stage, drumsticks in one hand, mixed drink in the other. His eyes were swimming in their sockets and rimmed with red. He was a big guy, on the short side, but ripped—the kind of guy Sam would usually imagine could hold his liquor. Clearly, however, Johnny was not an accomplished drinker.

"Dude! You are the *man*!" Johnny shouted, practically tackling Aidan out of his chair as he hugged him.

"How drunk *are* you?" Aidan asked, slapping Johnny's back.

"Very. I get performance anxiety," Johnny answered over his shoulder. "But I'm so glad you're here, man!"

Aidan shot Charlie a look that said, *This is why I dragged you here.* Charlie and Jeff laughed as the hug continued, and Sam found himself looking over his shoulder again, this time toward the door.

He should have asked Gaia to come with him tonight. He'd thought about it when he'd seen her earlier, but something had stopped him. Just like something had stopped him from bringing up the messages he'd left her. And the longer he'd said nothing about it, the longer she'd said nothing about it, and the more awkward it felt to even *think* about bringing it up.

The problem was, not saying something about it made him seem like he was embarrassed about it, which he was. Too embarrassed to jump straight to asking her out.

I'm just going to have to give it some time. Not a lot. Just some, Sam thought, taking another gulp of his beer. Once the memory of the many messages had faded a bit, he'd just call her up and ask her if she wanted to get together. Do something normal. Like go to the movies or for a walk. Or maybe a game of chess in the park. That was how they'd met, after all. It would be kind of romantic.

"Earth to Sam!" Aidan said, snapping in front of his face. He was standing up next to Sam now and Johnny had returned to his seat behind the drums. "What the hell are you thinking about?"

Just wondering what Gaia's doing right now, Sam's mind replied.

"Nothing," he answered.

"You've been zoning out all day," Aidan said. "I'm surprised you figured out how to put your pants on to come here."

"It's the chick stare," Jeff said, sucking at his teeth. "He's got the chick stare."

"What the hell are you talking about?" Charlie asked with a laugh. Jeff was always saying stupid, pointless crap with this serious intonation like it was all deep.

"He's thinking about some girl," Jeff said, rather astutely for him. "It's all over his face."

Charlie, Aidan, and Jeff all looked at Sam expectantly. Like he was really going to get into a detailed conversation about his "chick stare" and the object of it with these guys in the middle of a loud club. Not likely.

"You are so off base, you're halfway to the out-field," Sam said. "I'm just trying to remember whether we remembered to pause the Xbox before we left."

"Aw, dude, you better have remembered!" Jeff cried, moving to the edge of his seat. "I was like five minutes from slaying the dragon!"

"In your dreams," Charlie said.

Sam smiled. His friends were fabulously distractable.

"So, you want another beer or what?" Aidan asked, whacking Sam's shoulder with the back of his hand.

"Still working on this one," Sam answered, tilting the bottle toward his friend.

As Aidan walked to the bar, Sam tried to tune in to Charlie and Jeff's conversation—something about the club they wanted to hit later. The band hadn't started playing yet, but the music on the sound system was still pretty loud. Sam could barely hear what anyone was saying, and he knew once the band began their set, it would become impossible. Then he could zone out all he wanted.

Zone out and think of what to say when he asked out Gaia.

GAIA LOOKED DOWN AT THE BEEFY, outstretched hand of the human boulder sitting by the door at CB's Gallery and frowned. He grunted at her.

The Usual Angst

"What?" she asked.

"You gonna pay the cover?" the guy asked, his voice a low rumble. "Ten bucks."

"Oh!" Gaia said, her face heating up instantly. She fumbled in her bag, feeling completely unsophisticated and stupid—a sensation only exacerbated when two Spider-Man lollipops fell out onto the floor. She'd never actually been inside one of these places before. How was she supposed to know what it meant when some freaky tattoo-covered bouncer grunted in her direction?

"I got it," Jake said as Gaia crouched to retrieve her candy. He'd slapped a twenty into the guy's palm before Gaia had located her wallet.

Damn, she thought as he tugged at her arm and dove into the thick crowd. *He paid again.* She was really going to have to get a handle on this stuff. Gaia's brain was brimming with street smarts, but certain `way-of-the-world logic` completely mystified her.

Jake made his way toward the bar and Gaia followed. Suddenly, he stopped, blocked by a tight crowd of people, and Gaia took the opportunity to get a look around. The back part of the club, by the door, was an open area with couches and tables pushed up against the walls. The room was painted white, and there was actual artwork hanging on the walls. All the little tables had votive candles flickering inside white cups.

Gaia was just noticing this when she saw a booted foot flying toward one of the candles and she instinctively went to shout a warning. But before she could get the words out, she looked up and saw that the boot belonged to that Kai girl she'd seen Ed hanging around with. And the reason it was flying toward the candle was because she was crawling all over Ed himself on a love seat near the wall.

You have to be kidding me, Gaia thought, instantly turning her face away. He hadn't seen her yet and maybe he wouldn't recognize the back of her head, what with all the uncharacteristic waves in her hair. *Of all the bars and clubs in this town, why did he have to be here?*

Suddenly, her unusual night of fun was infused with a bit more of her usual angst.

Jake finally broke through and made it to the bar and Gaia stepped up next to him, putting more bodies between herself and her ex. There was a red Dust Magnets flyer plastered to a support beam and suddenly Gaia remembered where she'd seen it before.

"These things were all over school yesterday," she said as Jake tried to get the bartender's attention.

"Yeah, like I said, they're everywhere. I think a lot of people are coming," Jake said.

You said they were everywhere in Brooklyn, Gaia thought, irritated by the triangular situation she suddenly found herself in. All she wanted to do was get the heck out of there.

Then, as the people down at the other end of the bar got their drinks and moved away, Gaia saw something that *really* made her want to get the heck out of there. Sam Moon was sitting a few yards away, staring off into space.

"Oh, come on," Gaia said out loud, her heart turning.

"I know. This guy's not giving me the time of day," Jake replied, motioning at the frazzled bartender. "What do you want, anyway?" he asked Gaia.

"Nothing," Gaia said, her pulse racing. Sam was going to turn around any second and see her here with Jake. Or Ed was going to come over to get a drink. And she really wasn't sure she could handle either of those scenarios.

What had made her think that she could get away with one normal, fun night? Didn't she know the fates were working against her here? This couldn't be a coincidence. It was *too* coincidental. Someone was definitely pulling the strings up there and he or she had a sadistic sense of humor.

"Hey, Jake? Do you think we could—"

Gaia never finished her sentence because at that moment, one of the guitars on stage let out a screech that pierced the eardrums of everyone in the room. Jake didn't hear a word of what she'd said.

A few moments later, Jake had a soda in his hand and he grabbed Gaia's wrist with the other. As they wove their way back through the crowd, Gaia saw Ed recognize them from out of the corner of her eye. And when Jake plopped down into a chair near the stage, Sam noticed them, too.

Gaia looked back through the bar toward the door, past dozens and dozens of heads that were bopping up and down to the music. She looked at Jake, whose eyes were trained on the stage. There was no way to make a fast escape. If she got up and bolted, either Jake or Ed or Sam would catch up to her before she even made it halfway to the door. Or *all* of them would. There was no doubt about it. Gaia was trapped.

Swallowing against her dry throat, she sank down as low as possible in her chair, rested her elbow on the table and shielded her face with her hand. This night was about to get interesting.

To: Y
From: X22
Subject: Damage control

Have contacted our agent within the CIA. Agent
is in position to neutralize the prisoners before
you can be compromised. Agent awaits your orders.

To: X22
From: Y
Subject: Re: Damage control

Negative. Neutralization is too dangerous. We
must proceed carefully at this juncture.

My transfer to the new location is complete.
Safe house secure. It's time to go on the offen-
sive. Put together a team and take the girl.

"Yuri, my uncle, your beloved Katia's father, is very much alive, Tom," Natasha said firmly. "And he's here."

the bomb

ED STOOD NEAR THE WALL, BEHIND

Lost-Puppy-Dog Style

the area where the tables and chairs were set up, but in front of the crowd that was packed in behind them. Next to him, Kai bounced up and down, screaming and cheering—singing along to words that Ed couldn't remotely understand. The audience, for the most part, seemed to be enjoying the piercingly loud, repetitive set that the Dust Magnets were putting forth, but to Ed, it was torture. Every once in a while, if he could manage it without being obvious, he would press his fingertips into his ears to dull the noise and catch a bit of a reprieve.

Of course, he wasn't the only person in the room feeling tortured. Gaia was clearly ready and willing to be sucked into the ninth ring of hell. Every few seconds she seemed to be sinking a little bit lower in her chair until her knees were practically touching the ground. Jake, God bless him, was sitting slightly in front of her, watching the band, so he had yet to notice his date's—was it a date?—obvious distress.

At the same time, Sam was getting his stares in, lost-puppy-dog style. While his friends shouted and laughed to one another across the table, Sam sat back, eyeing Gaia, all droopy and sad.

Who is that guy? his look read. *Why is she here with him and not me?*

Ed had heard those thoughts in his own head more times than he cared to remember. He recognized his lost-puppy-dog expression. When it came to Gaia, he *invented* the lost-puppy-dog face. Seeing it on someone else only made him realize how pathetic he'd been for the past year. Why hadn't somebody smacked him upside the head and told him to snap the hell out of it?

Suddenly, Ed was struck with an idea. No one had done that for him, but that didn't mean he couldn't do it for someone else. It would be like philanthropy on a Saturday night. It might make the agony of this evening worthwhile.

"I'll be right back!" he shouted in Kai's ear. She smiled and nodded, continuing to bounce.

Ed made his way along the front of the crowd and over to Sam's table. He pulled a free chair from the next table, turned it around, and straddled it right at Sam's elbow.

"What's up, man?" Ed said.

Sam glanced at him, almost startled.

"Hey!" he shouted back with a nod. He took a sip of his beer and trained his eyes on the hideousness on the stage as if that was what he'd been watching all along.

"Look, Sam. I came over here to tell you that it's game over," Ed shouted, leaning in toward Sam's ear.

"What?" His eyebrows shot up and came together.

"Game over," Ed said, lifting his chin in Jake's direction. Sam followed his eyes, drawn back to the car wreck.

"I have no idea what you're talking about," Sam said.

But the defiant way in which he said it told Ed that he knew *exactly* what he was talking about. Still, it couldn't hurt to hammer it home.

"You see that guy she's with?" Ed said, leaning in again. "That's him. That's the guy with all the mojo you and I will never have." Ed reached up and clapped Sam on the shoulder in solidarity with his former adversary. "It's time to give it up, man," he said. "Trust me. I know."

Territorial

THIS HAS TO BE OVER SOON, GAIA thought, her head pounding as the band's front man executed some kind of wide-legged jump and almost took out the drummer's cymbals and dead-legged the bass man. *If there is any mercy in the world, this has to be over soon.*

"I'll be back in a minute!" Jake suddenly shouted at her.

Gaia sat up straight and grabbed his arm before

she could double-think it. "What? Where are you going?"

"Bathroom!" Jake yelled, starting out of his chair.

Gaia glanced in Sam's direction from the corner of her eye. Was it her imagination or was Ed just getting up from Sam's table?

"Why?" Gaia blurted.

Jake laughed. "I think it's kind of obvious. I'll be right back." Then he stepped away from the table, carefully avoiding wires and abandoned beer bottles.

Gaia suddenly felt like every light in the club was trained directly on her. *She's right here! Come and get her!*

Sam was watching her. She could feel it. She'd felt it all night long, but now it somehow seemed more intense. Her first instinct was to sink down in her chair again, but that wasn't going to get her anywhere. It wasn't going to make her disappear. Besides, her butt hurt from the edge of the seat pressing into it all night.

There was movement. Definite movement caught in her peripheral vision. Gaia cleared her throat and fixed her gaze on the band. She loved this band. She was *so* into them. She couldn't take her eyes off of them.

Yeah, right.

"Hey," Sam said, lurking just behind her shoulder. "Mind if I sit?"

Gaia pressed her lips together in a reasonable facsimile of a smile. "No extra chairs," she said pseudo-apologetically.

102

Sam leaned over to the couple next to them, pointing at an empty seat at their table. Seconds later, he was at eye level right across from her. Gaia glanced automatically in the direction of the bathrooms, but Jake was nowhere to be found.

"So, who's the guy?" Sam asked bluntly.

"Jake," Gaia replied, thankful that the deafening noise made it next to impossible to attempt to expand.

"Ah," Sam replied, nodding and looking around. As if the word "Jake" explained everything. He was playing it cool. Gaia could have kissed him for his male ego that required that he play it cool.

"So, listen. I've decided I'll talk to Oliver," Sam shouted, leaning in slightly.

Gaia's heart skipped a beat. "Yeah? That's great!" she shouted back.

Sam's green eyes took on new depth as he watched her face. "Yeah, well, it means a lot to you!" he yelled.

Gaia felt a stirring in her chest. So he was doing it for her. Not because he wanted to, not to help Oliver, but for her. Time for a subject change. Luckily, at that moment, the song ended, making it much easier to talk. Everyone cheered and applauded, and the front man told them all that it was time for the Dust Magnets' break.

"So," Gaia said. "I went to see Dmitri this morning."

"Yeah? I meant to ask you about that. It's weird, isn't it?" Sam said.

"What's weird?" Gaia asked.

"How he just up and split. I hope nothing's wrong," Sam said. "But then, with that guy—"

Gaia shook her head, confused. "What do you mean he up and split? I just saw him."

"Oh, he was there?" Sam said, adjusting in his seat. "Well, did he mention anything to you about where he was going, cuz he wasn't there this afternoon. . . ?"

"Sam," Gaia said, leaning forward. "What the hell are you talking about?"

"Okay, all I know is, I went over there this afternoon to get the last of my stuff, and when I got there most of Dmitri's stuff was gone—"

"And you don't know where he went?" Gaia asked, her voice rising.

"That's what I'm trying to tell you. I have no idea," Sam said. "He left me a note saying he'd be in touch and that was it."

"But I was *just* there." Gaia stood up from the table, her mind reeling. "Why didn't you call me? Why didn't you tell me this?"

"What? I just figured he was going off to do the laying low thing again," Sam said. "Ever since we busted Dmitri out he's been totally paranoid."

Gaia rolled her eyes to the ceiling and when she looked back at Sam, he seemed chagrined, like a little kid who'd just broken something expensive. "I just figured it was Dmitri being eccentric," he said. "Do you really think something's wrong?"

Gaia took a deep breath and told herself to chill. Maybe Dmitri really had gone off somewhere to stay under the radar. He'd done it before. But after the odd conversation she'd had with him that morning, something about his sudden disappearance just seemed off. Why wouldn't he have told her he was leaving?

At that moment, Jake emerged from around the corner and immediately noticed the new presence at their table. Gaia saw his face take on that terri-torial set as he made his way back a little faster than he'd left it. When his eyes met hers, he stopped in his tracks.

"What's wrong?" he asked, glancing down at Sam.

"We have to go," Gaia said.

"Whatever you say," Jake told her, coming around the table.

"Are you going over there?" Sam asked. "I can come if you—"

"No," Gaia interrupted a little more harshly than intended. Sam's mouth snapped shut and she instantly felt guilty. Not only was she leaving with another guy, she was rude to him in front of another guy—a major blow. Guys could be so fragile. But Gaia did not want to risk pulling Sam back into her crazy life again. "I'll let you know if we find anything," she told him.

And with that, she and Jake headed for the door.

TOM NEVER TOOK HIS EYES OFF

A Good Laugh

Natasha as he handed her the glass of water she requested. He sat down in his chair without looking at it or marking its position. He watched her and waited while she sipped from the cool, pristine glass and placed it down in front of her on the table. Tom was in charge this time. Nothing she could do or say would upset him.

"Thank you for moving Tatiana. These conversations, they're too difficult on her," Natasha said.

"You're welcome," Tom replied. He leaned back in his chair and crossed his legs, his ankle resting atop his knee. "So let's talk."

"How's Gaia?"

A surge of heat rushed up through Tom's body directly into his head. He fought the urge to glance at the one-way mirror, knowing Frenz was in there, observing him closely.

Just answer the question, Tom. No sarcasm.

"She's fine. But let's talk about you," Tom said. "For whom are you working?"

Natasha smiled slowly. "Jumping right in, Tom? You would rather not be here, I see. Is it because your colleagues gave me the deal you were so reluctant to offer?"

Tom uncrossed his legs, moved forward on his chair, and set his elbows on the table. It did bother him—the fact that his superiors had made a deal—but he wouldn't let that show. He looked deep into Natasha's eyes. "On the contrary, Natasha. There's no place I'd rather be. But you told my boss that you wanted to talk to me, and I'd appreciate it if you'd start talking."

She blinked, obviously surprised at his calm demeanor.

"Who sent you here?" he asked. "What was your primary mission? I know it wasn't to take Gaia out because you were here for months before you even attempted it."

Natasha gazed at him stonily. Tom started to lose his patience.

"Natasha, you're not stupid. You know they won't make good on your deal unless you give us some real intel," Tom said. "Why drag this out any longer? Why let Tatiana suffer any longer than she has to?"

She didn't move a muscle. She didn't even seem to be breathing. She sat like a statue for another few minutes before, finally, she opened her mouth and started to talk. Her voice was monotone, her expression resigned.

"Tom," she said. "I am Katia's cousin."

It was all he could do to keep from lifting a hand to his chest, which felt as if it had just been pierced through by a sword. Katia's cousin? *His* Katia?

"Not possible," he said, even as he saw the truth of the statement. His heart raced and he fought to control his emotions. Rosenberg and Frenz were watching, after all. He couldn't afford to lose it now.

"I know you always saw a resemblance. I know

107

that's why you were attracted to me. It's one of the reasons I was assigned to your case," Natasha continued in the same unaffected monotone.

It's one of the reasons I was assigned to your case. . . . This had to be wrong. This had to be a sick joke. How could anyone do this to another person—send his dead wife's cousin to seduce him—to exploit that weakness in his heart?

"Tatiana and I were sent to America to watch you. To keep an eye on you and see if you suspected what was going on within the Organization."

"The Organization," Tom repeated, adopting the same flat tone Natasha was using. If he didn't he was sure his myriad of emotions would show through, and he couldn't have that.

"You're not going to like this, Tom," Natasha said.

Tom narrowed his eyes at her. She was on the verge of telling him something. Something big. And from the triumphant look on her face, she was going to enjoy it.

"Okay, I'll bite," Tom said. "Who sent you? Who's running the Organization?"

Natasha lowered her chin and looked up at him through her lashes, her eyes gleaming. Time seemed to stop, but it hadn't. The only sound in the room was the ticking of Tom's watch.

"It is Yuri. My uncle. Katia's father. It was Yuri who sent us."

At that moment, Tom was glad to be sitting. His

every nerve and cell felt sick. Yuri Petrova could not be alive. Katia's evil psycho of a father could not be alive.

"Try again, Natasha," Tom told her, clear as a bell even as his hands shook under the table. "Yuri is six feet under and has been for years. We both know it."

"There have been many changes," Natasha continued as if Tom hadn't spoken at all. "Yuri is growing old and he needed a successor. Tatiana was being groomed to take over the Organization. But Yuri needed to be sure that you and Gaia would not get in the way. He needed to be sure that—"

Tom laughed. He couldn't help it. It was the only release he could allow himself. It burbled up through his chest and throat and pressed at his lips until he just couldn't hold it in any longer. Natasha stopped talking and stared at him.

"I'm sorry, I'm sorry," Tom said mirthfully. He pressed the top of his nose between his thumb and forefinger, then folded his hands on the table, his eyes still dancing. "It's just, I thought you were going to tell me the truth here tonight."

This couldn't be the truth. He refused to accept that.

"And I am," Natasha said blankly.

"You expect me to believe this?" Tom asked, standing abruptly, his chair scraping back across the concrete floor. He hovered over her, suddenly hyperaware of the eyes on him from the other side of the glass, hyperaware of the hammering of his own heart. "Natasha," he said, pressing his fingertips into the metal table and leaning over her. "Yuri has been dead for years."

Natasha leaned forward, the single light hanging above them casting distorted shadows across her face. She gazed up at him through her lashes, a coy smile playing on her lips. Whatever she was about to say, whatever bomb she was about to drop, she was enjoying it to the fullest.

"Yuri Petrova is very much alive, Tom," Natasha said firmly.

Tom swallowed. "I don't believe you."

"Well, you had better start," Natasha told him, cool and calm. "He is alive. And he is here."

"Here?" he repeated, searching her eyes. His body started to believe her before his brain did. The hairs on his arms stood on end and a chill shot through to his core. Natasha had lied to him before and he'd believed her, but this time she was telling the truth— the impossible, horrifying truth.

"He is in the U.S., Tom," Natasha told him, her smile widening at his obvious discomfort. "Yuri is here."

"OKAY, WHO IS THIS GUY AGAIN?"

Jake asked as he and Gaia climbed the stairs in Dmitri's building two at a time. They'd given up on the

Spooked

elevator after only two and a half minutes of waiting. Gaia and patience had parted ways hours ago.

"He's the one who helped me put Natasha in jail," Gaia told him, controlling her breathing as best she could. "And he wouldn't leave without telling me." Why would he tell her he'd always be there for her and then bolt the next minute without even a phone call? It wasn't like him.

"But that Sam guy said—"

"I know what he said," Gaia snapped, emerging onto Dmitri's floor. "And either he's wrong, or something's happened."

"Like what?" Jake asked, holding his side as he gasped for air. He was in great shape, but Gaia would bet it had been a long time since he'd taken fifteen flights of stairs at a sprint.

"I don't know! Maybe he was kidnapped! Maybe by the same people who took my father!" Gaia whispered hoarsely, growing frustrated. "That's what we're here to find out."

Gaia paused in front of Dmitri's door, took a deep breath, and knocked. There was no movement inside the apartment, no sound at all except the sound of Jake's rapid breathing behind her. She tried the knob—locked. Jake stepped aside as Gaia moved back, lifted her leg, and kicked in the door.

"Jesus!" Jake said as the locks ripped free from the wall. "Are you *trying* to get the neighbors to call the cops?"

Gaia couldn't even reply to his sarcasm. She was staring at what was left of Dmitri's apartment. This couldn't have been the same room she'd sat in just a few hours ago.

Drawers hung open, papers were strewn everywhere, a plant in the corner was overturned, a trail of clothing cut across the living room. The place was a total wreck.

"Something's not right," Gaia said flatly.

"Yeah, no kidding," Jake replied.

"Sam didn't say the place was trashed," Gaia told him, taking a couple of steps into the apartment. "He said Dmitri left a note. Somebody must have done this after Sam left."

"Like who?" Jake asked quietly.

"I don't know," Gaia said. "Someone's after him."

Then she heard a creak from a floorboard and before she could turn around, she and Jake were grabbed from behind.

You know what I need? I need to get out of here. I don't mean out of this bar or my school or my apartment. I need to get the hell out of this city. I need a college in a different state. Maybe a different country. I need to get as far away from here as possible, because one thing has become crystal clear to me: I am never going to fall out of love with Gaia as long as I have to see her every damn day. And as long as I'm still in love with her, no other girl has a shot. And as long as no other girl has a shot, I've got no shot.

No shot at love.

No shot at a functional relationship of any kind.

No shot of getting any play of any kind on any level.

Don't get me wrong. Sex isn't the only thing I think about. But I am a guy. A teenage guy. So it does occupy approximately

eighty percent of my conscious
thoughts. Maybe ninety. And when
Gaia's in the room, it's more
like ninety-nine.

When I'm with Kai, I can't
kiss her without thinking about
Gaia. And when Gaia's in my line
of vision when I'm with Kai, I
can't even focus on what the
girl is saying. I hate to admit
this, believe me. Kai deserves
better. She's an awesome girl
and I wish I could be the
boyfriend she deserves—for me
and for her. But when it comes
to girls of the non-Gaia variety
I am shit outta luck, as
they say.

So maybe if I go away—maybe
if I go to St. Louis or Seattle
or San Francisco, Paris or
Madrid or Minsk. Maybe if I
don't have to see her every day
I'll finally get her out of my
system. I'll finally be able to
focus my abundant sexual energy
on someone new. "Out of sight,
out of mind," right?

Or. . . wait . . . is it

"absence makes the heart grow fonder"?

    Damn.

    Why couldn't the proverb people just come up with one opinion and run with it?

"Why is
Yuri
here?"
Tom asked.
"He wants
Gaia," **the**
explanation
Natasha
replied.

Credible Threat

"SHE HAS TO BE LYING!" TOM asserted, his teeth clenched. "Yuri is dead. We know this."

Agents Rosenberg and Frenz watched Tom as he paced back and forth across the longer wall of the debriefing room. Director Vance stood in the corner, an intimidating presence, his arms crossed over his chest and his jowls working. No one present wanted Natasha's statement to be true. In his heyday, Yuri was considered to be a `credible threat` to the U.S. government. A serious danger to national security. He was on the international most wanted list. He was known for his ruthless tactics, his penchant for physical and emotional torture, his sadistic nature.

He was not a pleasant person to deal with.

"Agent Moore, I don't want to believe her any more than you do," Agent Rosenberg said, gripping her notebook. "But you and I both know she's exhibiting none of the signs of distress associated with lying. She hasn't blinked, she hasn't touched her face, she hasn't cleared her throat. We've been monitoring her body temperature with censors and—"

"I know, I know, it hasn't changed," Tom interrupted.

"And neither has her heart rate," Rosenberg finished, glancing down at her notes.

"Of course, we can't say the same for you, can we?" Agent Frenz asked stoically.

"Why don't you just say what you mean?" Tom demanded, feeling the truth of Frenz's insinuation. He was heating up even as he stood there.

"You almost lost your cool in there," Frenz pointed out. "Again."

"The woman just told me that my wife's psychotic, criminal mastermind father was still alive and that he had ordered surveillance on myself and my daughter. I think you can cut me the slightest bit of slack," Tom said, stepping up to Frenz. He was so close to the man he could see his already sizable nostrils flaring.

"Sir, I respectfully suggest that we remove Agent Moore from this case once and for all," Frenz said, taking a step back and looking at Director Vance. "I think we've given him enough chances to prove himself."

All eyes turned to Vance as he took a deep breath and rubbed his sizable hand over his face in frustration. Tom's throat was dry, but he forced himself to speak.

"I'm going back in there, sir," he said. "I have to finish this."

Vance inhaled again, drawing himself up to his full height. "Go," he said. "But tread lightly, Moore. You've been warned."

As Tom exited the room headed for the interrogation block, Frenz eyed him skeptically. Tom could have punched the little weasel.